TALES OF THE FANTASTIC

Broadwater House Poets in Prose series

Translations by Patricia Roseberry

A Season in Hell, Arthur Rimbaud
Artificial Paradise, Charles Baudelaire
Condemned, Victor Hugo
Tales of the Fantastic, Théophile Gautier
and others

Also translated by Patricia Roseberry
Incognito, Hervé Guibert

THEOPHILE GAUTIER
and others

TALES OF THE FANTASTIC

Translated by Patricia Roseberry

BROADWATER HOUSE

British Library Cataloguing in Publication Data
A catalogue record for this book is available
From the British Library

© Patricia Roseberry, 2000

ISBN 1-903121-02-7

This English translation published 2000 by
BROADWATER HOUSE
30 Park Parade Harrogate HG1 5AG

All rights reserved. No print of this publication may be reproduced, stored in a retrieval system or transmitted in any form or by any means, electronic, mechanical, photocopying, recording or otherwise, without prior permission in writing from the publishers Broadwater House.

CONTENTS

	PAGE
Translator's note	7

THEOPHILE GAUTIER
1. The Coffee Pot — 13
2. Omphale — 27
3. The Amorous Dead — 45
4. The Mummy's Foot — 97

GERARD DE NERVAL
The Hand of Glory — 119

GUILLAUME APOLLINAIRE
The Disappearance of Honoré Subrac — 183

CHRONOLOGIES
Théophile Gautier — 193
Gérard de Nerval — 198
Guillaume Apollinaire — 203

GLOSSARY
I Théophile Gautier — 213
II Gérard de Nerval — 222

TRANSLATOR'S NOTE

The *conte fantastique*, that form of short story whose great exponents Hoffman and Poe have always been very much admired in France, has its roots in the eighteenth century when such works as Horace Walpole's *Castle of Otranto* and Matthew Lewis' *The Monk* attracted a wide readership. In France, Cazotte's *The Devil in Love* (1772) is thought to be the first example of the genre.

In his analysis of the subject, *On the Fantastic in Literature*, Charles Nodier claims that all literature owes something to an element of the fantastic which he traces through Homer, Dante, Shakespeare and others. The fully-developed genre however, is one of the many flowers of the Romantic movement in French literature. Gautier and Nerval, both fervent admirers of Hoffman, used it is an outlet for all those tumultuous aspirations of a generation constrained by order, reason and morality - those rules and regulations which applied to art as well as to society.

The four Gautier stories included in this collection present, in the most charmingly appealing way and with a spice of humour, a quite formidable array of what, post-Freud, we have come to regard as complexes or psychoses of one form or another. Here are foot-fetishism and even necrophilia as well as a recurring theme of male passivity where a young inexperienced man is seduced by an incredibly beautiful and practised woman. In 'The Amorous Dead', the theme is vampirism, the myth of the (in this case) female undead seeking eternal life through her succession of lovers. We are at some distance from the gruesome fantasies of Poe, but Gautier's 'Amorous Dead' is as pure an example of the Double Personality syndrome as we are likely to meet outside Stevenson's Jekyll and Hyde. We can explore these fantasies safely, cushioned from the disturbing realities they enshrine by the author's decorative and entertaining presentation. Gautier likes to display his comprehensive knowledge of ancient history and of that period which seems to have been one of his favourites, the Regency, so that the trick of situating the stories in a vanished era also has the effect of protecting the reader from a genuine frisson of horror. These are not brooding, indeterminate Gothic nightmares but day-dreams leaving the dreamer to enjoy a sense of poignant, lingering regret.

Like Gautier, Nerval used the Part Works, publications appearing at regular intervals in which poems, essays and short stories, often serialised, made their début and were later collected in year books, to find a readership eager for the imagination-food supplied today by the cinema and television as well as the printed word. Nerval's 'Hand of Glory' was first published in the *Cabinet de Lecture* 24 September 1832, and it was in the same periodical the previous year that Gautier's 'Coffee Pot' appeared for the first time. Where Gautier is beguiling and allows the reader to bask in his world of alluringly supernatural sex, Nerval is challenging. Using to great effect the background of early seventeenth-century Paris, with a remarkable evocation of the old quarters of Les Halles, the Pré aux Clercs and the Pont Neuf, the 'Hand of Glory' is a satire in miniature where bourgeois respectability is held up to ridicule. Relying on old legends of magicians and alchemists which he is at pains to tell us were commonly-held beliefs at the beginning of the the seventeenth-century, and using, to add piquancy to the narrative, extracts from and references to that great store of pre-classical French literature of which Rabelais and Villon were the brightest stars, Nerval has constructed a brilliant entertainment all the more effective for the pace at which it moves. The four main characters, poor Eustache the draper's assistant, Maître Gonin the magician whose knowledge of the Black Arts seems to have been inherited from previous incarnations, the boastful arquebusier and most interesting of all, the old lawyer Maître Chevassut who expresses truly anarchic views on the function of the legal system, are as impressive a collection as any drawn from the great comic writers of French literature. But though 'The Hand of Glory' is richly comic, it seems, for the author, to have been oddly premonitory for he was destined to commit suicide by hanging, in the rue de la Vieille Lanterne, not far from the Châtelet, during one of his periodic fits of insanity.

Apollinaire's story 'The Disappearance of Honoré Subrac' has been included because it bears the hall-mark of the *conte fantastique* reduced, by the spareness of its style, to minimalist proportions. Its surrealist quality is exceptionally powerful: it is as strange and disturbing as a concept by Dali.

In addition to brief chronologies of the writers, a glossary has been provided for the benefit of those who might otherwise feel obliged to seek clarifying information from works of reference.

THE COFFEE POT

by Théophile Gautier
First published in *Le Cabinet de Lecture*,
May 1831

THE COFFEE POT

I

Last year I was invited to spend a few days at a country house in Normandy, with Arrigo and Pedrino, two friends from Art School.

The weather had been full of promise on our departure but it changed suddenly and so much rain fell that the tracks leading to the estate were like the bed of a torrent.

We trudged along with mud almost up to our knees. A thick layer of heavy clay stuck to the soles of our boots and slowed us down so much we did not arrive at our destination until nightfall.

We were tired out. Seeing how hard we tried to stifle our yawns and keep our eyes open, our host packed us off to bed as soon as we had had supper.

My room was huge. I shivered slightly as I went in, for I seemed to be entering a different world.

You would have thought you were back in the last century, during the Regency of Philippe of Orleans. Boucher panels representing the four seasons were set over the doors, the furniture was loaded with rococo objets d'art in the worst possible taste and the walls had been lavishly decorated with murals.

The room appeared to be still in use, for the dressing table was covered in an assortment of combs, boxes and powder puffs and two or three taffeta dresses lay on the well-polished floor together with a fan decorated with silver sequins. To my surprise, a tortoise-shell snuff-box full of fresh snuff lay open on the mantle-piece.

It was only after the servant had wished me goodnight having placed the candlestick on the bedside table, that I became aware of all this and the signs of recent occupation disturbed me a little. Undressing quickly, I lay down on the bed and turned my head to the wall in an attempt to dispel my foolish fears.

I found myself unable to remain for long in that position. The bed seemed to toss beneath me like a wave, my eyelids refused to stay shut. I felt compelled to turn over and take a look.

The fire cast red shadows round the room and you could clearly distinguish the characters in the tapestry and the faces in the smoky portraits hanging on the wall.

They were our host's ancestors: knights in armour, judges in their wigs, fine ladies with rouged cheeks and powdered hair each with a rose in her hand.

The fire blazed up suddenly and the room grew bright; I realised that what I had taken for lifeless paintings were nothing of the sort! Eyes moved and flashed, mouths opened and closed, like the mouths of people engaged in conversation, but all I heard was the ticking of the clock and the sighing of the autumn wind. The clock struck eleven. The last stroke reverberated for a very long time and when it had died away, I hardly dare say what happened next, for no one will believe me!

The candles lit themselves, the bellows picked themselves up and began to blow on the fire as if by an invisible hand, wheezing like an old man with asthma whilst the tongs moved about in the logs and the shovel scooped up the ashes.

A coffee pot got down from the table and limped over to the the hearth where it sat down among the cinders.

A few minutes later, the armchairs began to stir. Moving with surprising agility on their ornamental feet, they came to rest in a semi-circle round the fireplace.

II

I could make neither head nor tail of what I saw, but what remained to be seen was even stranger.

One of the portraits, the oldest of all, a jolly grey-beard who reminded me of Sir John Falstaff stuck his head out of the frame. With great difficulty he managed to persuade his shoulders and belly to do the same and jumped down heavily to the floor.

Scarcely had he drawn breath than he pulled from his pocket a remarkably small key. Blowing on it to clear away the dust, he used it on each of the frames in turn whereupon they all grew bigger to enable their occupants to get down. Florid little abbés, yellow skinned dowagers, grave magistrates enveloped in great black robes, young beaux in silk stockings and velvet breeches, their swords at the *garde à vous,* all these characters presented such a curious sight that I laughed in spite of my alarm.

These worthy people sat down and the coffee pot jumped lightly on to the table. They drank coffee out of Japanese blue and white porcelain cups which appeared of their own accord on the table from off the top of the bureau, each furnished with a sugar lump and a silver spoon.

When coffee had been taken, the cups, coffee pot and spoons disappeared all at once and the conversation began, the strangest conversation I have ever heard, for not one of the speakers looked at the others: all stared intently at the clock.

I could not take my eyes off the clock either and followed the slow movement of the pointer towards twelve.

Midnight struck at last. A voice of exactly the same timbre as the clock itself declared: 'Now it is time to dance'.

The entire company rose to its feet. The armchairs drew back of their own accord then each gentleman took the hand of a lady and the same voice said:

'Gentlemen of the orchestra, begin!'

I forgot to tell you that the subject of the tapestry was an Italian orchestra on one side and a stag hunt on the other, with the huntsmen sounding the horn. The horn players and the musicians who until then had given no sign of life bowed their heads in acknowledgement.

The conductor raised his baton and the musicians struck up a lively dance tune. First, the company danced the minuet.

But the rapid notes of the score played by the musicians did not match the stately movement of the dancers. After a while, each pair of dancers began to spin round and round like a top. The women's silk dresses made a curious noise as they whirled, like a flight of pigeons or a beating of wings. Puffed up from beneath by the draught, they looked like bells ringing.

The musicians' bows attacked the strings so vigorously that they struck sparks from them, the fingers of the flautists moved up and down like quicksilver, the huntsmen's cheeks swelled out like balloons and the resulting deluge of notes was so rapid and tumultuous that even the demons of hell could not have kept up the pace for more than a few seconds.

It was pitiful to see the efforts of the dancers as they jumped about and executed sweeps of the leg, jetés and entrechats three feet high. Sweat poured down their faces and carried away the little black patches and the rouge. Whatever they did, however hard they tried, the music was always three or four notes ahead of them.

The clock struck one. They stopped and I saw someone I had not noticed until then: a woman who was not dancing.

I had never seen anyone so beautiful, not even in my dreams. Her skin was dazzlingly white, her hair ash-blonde, she had long lashes framing eyes so blue, so transparent I could see her soul through them as clearly as you can see a pebble at the bottom of a stream.

If ever I fell in love it would be with her! Impulsively, I leapt to my feet and went over to her, taking one of her hands in mine. I found myself talking to her as if I had known her for twenty years.

Oddly enough, as I spoke to her I kept time with the music by nodding my head, for it had not stopped and although I was in the seventh heaven at conversing with such a beautiful creature I was dying to dance with her.

I did not dare to ask her but she seemed to understand what I wanted because she raised her hand towards the clock, saying: 'When the pointer is there, we shall see, my dear Théodore'.

I cannot explain why, but it was no surprise to me to hear her speak my name and we went on talking. At last the clock struck the hour and the silvery voice spoke again: 'You may dance with the gentleman, Angela, if you wish, but you know what will happen'.

21

'It doesn't matter', replied Angela in a sulky voice.

She put her ivory-pale arm around my neck.

'Prestissimo' cried the voice.

And we began to waltz. Her soft cheek brushed mine as I held her in my arms. My feelings were exactly as you can imagine. I was divinely happy and would have liked to go on dancing like that for ever although the speed of the orchestra had tripled. But we had not the slightest difficulty in keeping up with it.

Amazed at our skill, everyone clapped their hands with enthusiasm and cried 'bravo', yet no sound was heard as they did so.

Angela, who had waltzed with surprising agility and energy until then, suddenly appeared to tire. She hung on to my shoulders as if her legs were about to give way beneath her. Her little feet which until now had seemed to skim the floor were as heavy as lead.

'You are tired, Angela', I said. 'Let us take a rest'.

'Willingly', said she, wiping her brow with her handkerchief, 'but everyone sat down while we were dancing and there is only one armchair left. There are two of us'.

'No matter my angel. You will sit on my knee'.

III

Without making the slightest objection, Angela sat on my knee and her arms went round me like a white scarf. She laid her head on my breast to warm herself for she had grown as cold as ice.

I do not know how long we remained in this position. All my senses were absorbed in contemplating the mysterious, fantastic creature on my knee.

I had no idea where I was or what time it was. The real world no longer existed for me and all the bonds which had tied me to it were broken. My soul, released from its earthly prison, floated in paradise. I understood what no one else could even begin to understand - Angela's thoughts communicating themselves to me without need of words. Her soul shone through her body like a lamp in alabaster; her thought-rays pierced right through me.

But the lark sang and a pale glimmer of light appeared at the window.

As soon as she saw it, Angela got up hurriedly, made a gesture of farewell, took one or two steps then uttered a cry and fell down in a swoon.

I darted forward to gather her up in my arms ... my blood runs cold to think of it ... there was nothing there but the coffee pot, broken into a thousand fragments!

Convinced I was the victim of some diabolical illusion, I was filled with such terror that I lost consciousness.

IV

When I came to, I was in bed. Arrigo and Pedro were standing over me and as soon as I opened my eyes, Arrigo exclaimed: 'About time too! I've been rubbing your brow with cologne for the past half hour. Whatever happened to you last night?

'This morning, when you didn't come down for breakfast, I came in here and found you lying full length on the floor, dressed in funny old-fashioned clothes, clutching a piece of broken porcelain as if it were a pretty girl'.

'He's wearing my grandfather's wedding clothes!' said Pedrino, lifting up a rose-coloured silk basque patterned in green. 'Look, here are the rhinestone buttons he was always talking about. Theodore must have found them somewhere and put them on for fun. But what made you faint? That sort of thing is all very well for a fragile young lady - you loosen her laces, take off her scarf and her necklace...'

'It was just a moment of weakness', I said abruptly. 'It's happened before'. With that I got up and took off my ridiculous costume.

Then we went in to luncheon.

My three friends ate a lot and drank a great deal more. I hardly ate at all. The memory of what had happened, or what I thought had happened, made me strangely thoughtful.

After luncheon we could not go out as it was still pouring with rain. We amused ourselves as best we could - Pedrino drummed tunes on the window with his fingers, Arrigo and our host played draughts. I took a sheet of paper from my album and began to draw.

The features traced faintly by my pencil represented with wonderful accuracy the coffee pot which had played so important a part in the events of the previous night.

'It's amazing how much that head looks like my sister Angela', said the host, who had finished his game of draughts and was looking over my shoulder.

What had looked like a coffee pot a few minutes ago was in fact the sweet melancholy profile of Angela.

'Is she alive of dead?' I asked as intensely as if my life depended on his reply.

'She died two years ago, of a seizure, after attending a ball', was the answer.

Brushing away a tear, I replaced the drawing in my album and sighed, for I knew I could never be really happy again in this world.

OMPHALE, a rococo tale
by Théophile Gautier
First published in
Le Journal des Gens du Monde,
7 February 1834

OMPHALE, a rococo tale.

My uncle the Chevalier lived in a little house overlooking on one side the gloomy rue des Tournelles and on the other the equally gloomy boulevard Saint Antoine. Between the boulevard and the main building a few straggling hornbeams covered in moss and insects spread their meagre branches across a sort of dismal wilderness hemmed in by high black walls. Sickly-looking flowers hung their heads like consumptive young girls, waiting for a ray of sunlight to dry out their decaying leaves. Weeds had taken over the paths which could hardly be made out at all for it was a long time since they had seen a rake. One or two goldfish floated rather than swam in a pond choked with duckweed and marsh plants.

My uncle called that his garden.

In my uncle's garden, apart from all the beautiful things I have just described, there was a pavilion of somewhat cheerless appearance to which he had given the name 'les Délices', no doubt because it suggested exactly the opposite. It was in a state of total dilapidation. The walls buckled; large flakes of plaster had fallen off and were lying on the ground amid the nettles and rye grass; the base was green with damp; the shutters and the doors were warped so they no longer closed properly. An object like a big fire-basket decorated the main entrance, for at the time when 'les Délices' was built, in the reign of Louis XV, it was customary to have two entrances. The rain-soaked cornice, covered in scrolls and other decorative features was rotting away. Nothing could be more depressing than my uncle's pavilion.

That pathetic ruin of plaster, not stone, cracked and moss-grown and covered in mould was like one of those prematurely aged men ravaged and worn out by debauchery. It inspired no respect because there is nothing in the world as ugly and pitiful as an old muslin dress and an old plaster wall, two things that are not made to last but last all the same.

My uncle had arranged for me to sleep in the pavilion.

It was no less antiquated within than without, though in slightly better condition. The bed was upholstered in yellow silk with big white flowers. The ornamental clock was set on a pedestal encrusted with mother-of-pearl and ivory. A garland of rosebuds coquettishly encircled a Venetian mirror; above the doors were cameos representing the four seasons. A fine lady with powdered hair, a sky-blue bodice and ribbons to match, a bow in her right hand, a partridge in her left, her brow adorned with a crescent moon and a greyhound at her feet, preened and smiled in the most charming way possible within a wide oval frame. She was one of my uncle's old flames and he had had her painted as Diana. As you see, the furniture was not exactly modern. You had no reason not to believe that you were in the time of the Regency, and the mythological tapestry covering the walls completed the illusion. The tapestry depicted Hercules spinning at the feet of Omphale. The design was in the style of Vanloo, that is to say, highly elaborate and mannered. Hercules was holding a spindle adorned with a pink ribbon; he was crooking his little finger like a marquis taking a pinch of snuff and rolling a white skein of thread between his thumb and index finger. His sinewy neck was hung about with ribbon bows, rosettes, strings of pearls and a myriad articles of feminine jewellery. A wide skirt with enormous panniers made of shot silk completed the heroic dragon-slayer's courtly disguise.

Omphale's white shoulders were half-concealed beneath the hero's Nemean lion skin. Her slender hand rested on her lover's knotty cudgel; her lovely ash-blond hair, lightly veiled in powder, hung nonchalantly down her neck which was as graceful as a dove's. Her little feet, the feet of a Spanish or Chinese lady, too small even for Cinderella's slipper, were shod in buskins, pale lilac with a scattering of pearls. How charming she looked! She held her head back in an attitude of adorable boldness, her lips were pursed in a delicious little pout; her nostrils flared slightly and her cheeks were rather flushed. Cunningly placed, a black taffeta patch brought out the brilliance of her complexion. All she lacked, to complete the impression of a young musketeer, was a small moustache.

There were many other characters in the tapestry: the obligatory lady's maid, the conventional cupid, but they left no particular impression on my memory for me to be able to describe them.

At that time I was very young, which does not mean that I am very old now, but I had just completed my education and I was staying with my uncle until I had decided on a profession. If the old man had been able to predict that I would become a teller of fantastic tales he would doubtless have shown me the door and disinherited me. For literature in general and writers in particular he expressed the most aristocratic disdain. Like the real gentleman he was, he would have flogged all those little scribblers who spend their time making black marks on paper and making fun of persons of quality. May my poor uncle's soul rest in peace.

I had just left school. I was full of dreams and illusions. I was as naive as Candide. Delighted to have no more essays to write I thought everything was for the best in the best of all possible worlds. I believed in a great many things: I believed in Aesop's fables; I really thought there were nine muses... My literary studies had created for me a little world where everything was pink, sky blue and apple green. As Mephistopheles says in Faust: holy innocence!

When I found myself with this lovely room all

to myself I was in the seventh heaven. I carefully noted every single item of furniture, ferreted about in every corner, explored every nook and cranny. After supper, (at my uncle's you had *supper,* a charming custom that has died out along with so many others no less charming that I regret with all my heart), I took my candle and retired, so impatient was I to enjoy my new home.

As I undressed, I had the impression that Omphale's eyes moved. I looked more closely, not without a shiver of fear, for the room was large and the faint light shed by my candle only made the darkness more visible. I thought her head was turned the other way. Fearfully, I blew out the light. I turned towards the wall, pulled the sheet over my head, my night-cap down to my chin and fell asleep at last.

It was several days before I dared take another look at the tapestry.

To make the unlikely story I am about to tell more likely, it might be a good idea to inform my fair readers that at that time I was indeed a good-looking lad. I had the most beautiful eyes in the world (I say this only because someone once said it to me), a slightly fresher, more peach-like complexion than I have today, dark curly hair (which I still have) and I was seventeen years of age. All I lacked was a pretty countess to turn me into a very passable Cherubino... unfortunately, the only countess I knew was fifty-five with three teeth, too much on the one hand and not enough on the other.

One evening, however, I worked myself up to the point of taking a look at Hercules' lovely mistress. She stared at me with the saddest, most languorous look you can imagine. This time, I pulled my night-cap down to my shoulders and put my head under the bolster.

That night I had a strange dream, if that is what it was.

I heard the curtain rings round my bed slide and jingle as if the draperies had suddenly been tweaked apart. I woke up, or at least it seemed in my dream that I woke up. There was no one to be seen.

The moon was shining in through the window, casting a pale blue light around the room. Great shadows and fantastic shapes were projected on to the floor and the walls. The clock struck the quarter; its vibration was prolonged, like a sigh.

The tick of the clock could be heard quite distinctly and resembled the heart-beat of a person labouring under some strong emotion.

A sudden squall of wind shook the windows and rattled the shutters. The woodwork creaked and the tapestry stirred. I risked a glance at Omphale, suspecting she had something to do with all this. I was not mistaken.

The tapestry began to shake violently. Omphale detached herself from the wall and jumped lightly down to the floor. She came over to my bed, taking care to turn the right way round. It is unnecessary to describe my amazement. The most intrepid old warrior would have been ill at ease in such a situation and I was neither old nor a warrior. I waited with bated breath for the next stage of the adventure.

A sweet silvery voice sounded in my ear, with that prettily affected throaty 'r' adopted by marquises and people of Society during the Regency. 'Are you afraid of me, child? It is true you are only a child but it isn't nice to be afraid of ladies, especially when they are young and wish you no harm. It isn't chivalrous and it isn't French. Get rid of those fears. Come on, ill-mannered little boy, don't look like that, and take your head out of the bed-clothes. Your education is by no means complete. You are not exactly precocious; in my day, Cherubinos were much bolder than you'.

'But madame ...'

'It seems strange to see me here and not over there, I agree', she said, biting her red lower lip with her white teeth and pointing a long slender finger towards the wall. 'It isn't natural, I agree, but if I explained it to you, you wouldn't understand it any better. Just remember you are not in any danger'.

'I'm afraid you could be the ... the ...'

'The devil? Be honest. That's what you mean. At least you will agree that I'm not too black, for a devil, and if hell were populated with devils like me the time would be spent as pleasantly as in paradise'.

To prove she was not boasting, Omphale cast off her lion skin to reveal shoulders and bosom that were perfectly shaped and of dazzling whiteness.

'What do you think now?' she asked, with self-satisfied coquettishness.

'That if you were the devil himself I would no longer be afraid, Madame Omphale!

'That's more like it, but don't call ne *madame* or *Omphale*. I do not wish to be *madame* for you and I an no more *Omphale* than I am the devil'.

'Who are you then?'

'I am the Marquise de T***. Shortly after my marriage, the marquis had this tapestry made for my apartment; the artist portrayed me in the costume of Omphale. My husband is depicted as Hercules, heavens knows why - no one was less like Hercules than the poor marquis. This room has not been lived in for a very long time. I, who adore company, was bored to death. To be with one's husband is to be alone. When you turned up, I was delighted. This dead room came to life again. I had someone to interest me. I watched your comings and goings, observed you sleeping and dreaming. I took note of what you read. I found you charming and attractive: I fell in love with you. I tried to gain your attention. I sighed and you thought it was the wind. I gazed longingly at you, beckoned to you, but all I managed to do was alarm you. In despair, I decided on this course of action, unusual as it is. I made my mind up to tell you out loud what you could not understand when I merely hinted at it. Now you know I love you, I hope that ...'

The conversation had just reached this stage when suddenly a key rattled in the lock.

Omphale started and blushed to the roots of her hair.

'Farewell!' she whispered, 'till tomorrow'. She returned to her wall backwards, for fear of letting me see her other side.

It was Baptiste coming to fetch my clothes to brush them.

'Monsieur should not sleep with the curtains open', he said. 'Monsieur could catch cold. This room is very chilly'.

The bed curtains were, in fact, open and I was very surprised as I was sure they had been closed in the evening and besides, I thought I was dreaming.

As soon as Baptiste had gone, I hurried over to the tapestry. I felt it all over: it was a real tapestry made of wool, harsh to the touch, like all tapestries. Omphale was as much like the charming ghost of the night as a corpse is like a living being. I raised the fabric to look behind it but the wall was unbroken, neither a secret door nor a sliding panel. I merely noticed that there were several broken threads in the area where Omphale's feet touched the ground. That made me think.

For the whole of that day I remained in a state of total self-absorption. I awaited the evening with a mixture of anxiety and impatience. I went to my room early, dying to find out what would happen. I went to bed. The marquise was not long in putting in an appearance. She jumped down from the wall and came straight over to my bed. She sat down at the head and the conversation began.

As I had done the night before, I asked her questions and demanded explanations.

She avoided the first and answered the others evasively but with so much wit that an hour later I had no scruples about my liaison with her.

As she spoke to me she ran her fingers through my hair, stroked my cheeks playfully and kissed me lightly on the forehead.

She prattled on in a way that was mocking and beguiling, in a style at one and the same time elegant, familiar and utterly aristocratic. I have never come across that style again in anyone.

At first she was sitting on the chair next to the bed. Soon she put an arm round my neck and I felt her heart beating fast against mine. A delightful and beautiful woman was here with me, a real live marquise! And I a poor schoolboy of seventeen! Enough to make anyone lose his head. I lost mine, I had very little idea of what was about to happen but I suspected the marquis would be none too pleased.

'What will monsieur the marquis say, over there on his wall?'

The lion skin was on the ground and the pale lilac buskins were on the floor next to my slippers.

'He won't say anything', said the marquise with a tinkling laugh. 'Does he ever say anything? Even if he did, he is the most philosophical and inoffensive husband in all the world. Do you love me, child?'

'Oh yes, very much ...'

Day broke and my mistress took her leave of me.

The day seemed unbearable long. Night came at last. The same thing happened again and the second night was even better than the first. The marquise became more and more adorable. And

41

so it went on, for quite some time. But as I did not sleep at night, I was afflicted by day with a somnolence which aroused the suspicions of my uncle. He began to smell a rat. He probably listened outside the door and had heard everything. One fine morning he came into my room so suddenly that Antoinette hardly had time to get back into her place on the wall. He was accompanied by an upholsterer carrying pliers and a ladder.

The way he looked at me, severely and with disapproval, told me he knew everything.

'That marquise de T*** is completely mad. What possessed her to fall in love with such a brat?' muttered my uncle. 'She promised to behave herself! Jean, take down that tapestry, roll it up and put it in the attic'.

Every word he uttered was a dagger in my heart.

Jean rolled up my lover Omphale (or the marquise Antoinette de T***) together with Hercules, (or the marquis de T***), and carried them up to the attic. I could not restrain my tears.

The next day my uncle sent me back in the stage coach to my respectable parents to whom I uttered not a word about my adventure, as you can imagine.

My uncle died. They sold his house and all the furniture. The tapestry was no doubt sold along with all the rest.

Nevertheless, some time ago, as I was ferreting about in an antiques shop, looking for party masks and disguises, I stumbled against a dusty old bundle full of spiders' webs.

'What's that?' I asked the dealer.

'It's an eighteenth century tapestry representing the amours of Madame Omphale and Monsieur Hercules. It's genuine Beauvais, all silk and very well preserved. Buy it for your study. I'll let you have it cheap, seeing it's you'.

At the name of Omphale, all the blood seemed to drain out of my body.

'Unroll that tapestry!' I cried feverishly.

It was she. Her mouth seemed to smile graciously at me and her eyes kindled on meeting mine.

'How much do you want for it?'

'I cannot let you have it for less than four hundred francs'.

'I haven't that much on me. I'm off to fetch it now and I'll be back within the hour!'

I returned with the money but the tapestry had

gone, purchased, it seems by an Englishman who paid six hundred francs for it.

Perhaps it was better things turned out that way and I kept a fragrant memory intact. They say one should never go back to one's first love or revisit the rose one admired yesterday.

And after all. I am no longer young enough or handsome enough for tapestries to come down off the wall for me.

THE AMOROUS DEAD
by Théophile Gautier
First published in *Le Chronique de Paris,*
23 and 26 June 1836

THE AMOROUS DEAD

by Théophile Gautier

First published in 1836 under the title
La Morte Amoureuse

THE AMOROUS DEAD

You ask me, my friend, if I have ever loved. Yes indeed! My story is strange and terrible; even now, at the age of sixty-six, I can scarcely bring myself to stir the ashes of memory. To you I will tell all, but I would shrink from relating a tale like mine to a less experienced man. The events I am about to describe are so strange I can hardly believe they happened at all.

For more than three years I was the victim of a singular and diabolical illusion. I, a poor country priest, led nightly, in my dreams - and may God grant they were dreams - the life of a degenerate libertine. A single careless glance at a woman nearly brought about my damnation but at last, with God's grace and the help of my patron saint I succeeded in driving away the evil spirit that possessed me. In the day-time I was a priest, chaste, devoted to a life of prayer and sacred things. At night, as soon as my eyes were closed, I became a young nobleman, a connoisseur of women, dogs and horses, a gambler and a rake. When I woke at dawn it seemed to me I was asleep and that I was dreaming I was a priest.

From this nocturnal life I have retained memories of objects and words I cannot erase and although I have never been outside the four walls of a presbytery you would think me a man who, having exhausted the flesh-pots, has turned at last to religion and wishes to end his days under the sheltering wing of God's forgiveness rather than a humble seminarist who has grown old in an obscure parish in the depths of the country without any knowledge of the outside world.

Oh yes, I have loved as no one has ever loved before, with an insane and violent passion...

From earliest childhood I had a vocation for the priesthood. All my studies tended in that direction and until I was twenty-four my life was one long novitiate. After theological college I rose through all the minor orders in turn until at last my superiors judged me worthy, in spite of my youth, of taking the last decisive step. The day of my ordination was fixed for Holy Week.

I had no experience of the world. My existence was bounded by the seminary and the ecclesiastical college. I was vaguely aware of something called *woman* but I never gave it any thought. I was perfectly innocent. I saw my mother, who was old and infirm, only twice a year. She was my only link with the world outside.

I had no regrets. I felt no hesitation before this irrevocable commitment, I was full of impatience and joy. No young fiancé ever counted the days with more feverish longing. I could not sleep. I dreamed I was celebrating the Mass. To be a priest seemed the most desirable thing in all the world. I would have refused a king's throne or a poet's laurels. My ambition went no further than the priesthood. I tell you these things so you will understand how what happened to me should never have happened and how inexplicable was the fascination to which I fell victim.

When the great day came at last, I went to church with so light a step I felt I was walking on air or borne aloft by wings. I thought I was an angel and was surprised to see the dark preoccupied looks of my companions. There were many of us. I had spent the night in prayer and was in a state bordering on ecstasy. The bishop was a venerable old man who looked like God the Father contemplating eternity. I could see heaven through the vault of the temple.

No doubt you are acquainted with the details of

the ceremony: benediction, communion of bread and wine, anointing of the hands and finally the sacrifice offered in concert with the bishop. I will not linger over these matters. But how right was Job when he said: 'Foolish is the man who does not make a covenant with his eyes'... I raised my head which until that instant I had held bowed, and beheld, so close to me it seemed I could have touched her although she was in fact some distance away on the other side of the aisle, a young woman of singular beauty dressed with royal magnificence. It was as if scales fell from my eyes. I was like a blind man who suddenly recovers his sight. The bishop in his splendid vestments paled into insignificance, the candles dimmed in their sconces like stars at daybreak and the whole church grew dark. The heavenly creature stood out against that sombre background like a vision of loveliness. She seemed to give out light of herself rather than to receive it.

I lowered my gaze determined to avoid distraction for my attention was wandering so much I hardly knew what I was doing.

A moment later I opened my eyes again for I could see her through my lashes, sparkling with the colours of a prism against a dark background. It was like looking at the sun.

How beautiful she was. The greatest painters searching for an ideal beauty who created portraits of the Madonna came nowhere near this fabulous reality. Neither the verses of the poets nor the palette of a painter could give any idea of it. She was tall, with the bearing of a goddess. Her blonde hair flowed down on either side her face in golden cascades - she was a queen wearing her crown. Her forehead, white and blue-veined at the temples was wide and serene above eyebrows arched and almost dark, a singularity which added to the intensity of sea-green eyes of incomparable depth and sparkle. Such eyes! One flash could decide a man's destiny. I had never seen such brilliance and fire in human eyes before; they sent out arrows which pierced my heart. Whether from heaven or hell, that fire surely came from one or the other. That woman was an angel or a devil, perhaps both. She could not have been born of mother Eve. Her white teeth sparkled in their red smile, the proud curve of her nose suggested royal lineage, her shoulders gleamed whitely and a necklace of pearls of the same whiteness encircled her neck. From time to time she moved her head with the undulating motion of a snake or a feeding peacock, which set quivering the finely embroidered collar of her dress which was of red velvet. From its wide ermine-lined sleeves emerged hands of a patrician delicacy with long fine fingers as transparent as Aurora's.

I recall these details as if it were yesterday and though I was deeply disturbed, nothing escaped my notice, not the slightest nuance nor the little beauty spot on the point of the chin, the down on the upper lip, the velvet texture of the brow, the quivering shadow of the lashes on the cheek. I perceived everything with astonishing clarity.

As I watched her, new vistas opened before me. Life took on a different meaning. I had just been re-born to a new order of ideas. Such anguish gripped my heart I felt each minute go by either with the speed of a second or at the snail's pace of a century. But the sacred ritual continued, although I was now being carried away so far from the world I had lately wished to enter.

I said 'yes' when I meant 'no', when everything within me protested at the violence my tongue was doing to my soul. Some occult power tore the words of acquiescence from my lips: perhaps this is why so many young women go to the altar determined to refuse the husband they are being forced to accept but can never find the courage to do so. No doubt this is why so many poor novices take the veil although they feel they could tear it to pieces the minute they have pronounced their vows - how could they cause such a scandal or disappoint so many people? All those eyes, all those high expectations are like a dead weight impossible to shift and everything has been so well prepared in advance, in such an irrevocable way that the heart quails and yields unconditionally.

The expression of the beautiful stranger changed in the course of the ceremony. From tender and loving it became disdainful and discontented, as if she had been misunderstood.

I made a supreme effort to cry out that I did not wish to become a priest, but failed. My tongue stuck to the roof of my mouth and I was unable to express my desire by even the slightest show of refusal. I was in that state of waking nightmare when it is impossible, though one's life depends on it, to utter a single word.

She seemed to be aware of the torture I felt and

as if to encourage me threw me a glace expressive of heavenly promise. Her eyes were a poem. She seemed to say: 'If you will be mine, I will make you happier than God Himself in Paradise. The angels will envy you. Cast aside the shroud you are about to put on. I am beauty, I am youth. Come to me and we will be love itself. What could Jehovah offer you in compensation? Our life will be a dream of delight.

'Refuse the wine of this chalice and you are free. I will take you to the islands of the unknown. You will sleep on my breast in a great golden bed beneath a silver tent. I love you and wish to take you from your God at whose feet so many noble hearts cast oceans of love that never reach Him'.

I seemed to hear these words uttered to a rhythm of infinite sweetness for her gaze almost became the sound of music and the words her eyes sent out to me vibrated in my innermost heart as if an invisible mouth had whispered them into my soul. I was ready to renounce God although my heart mechanically went through the formalities of the ceremony. The lovely creature threw me a second glance of such desperation that I felt my heart pierced, like Our Lady of Sorrows, by many swords.

It was finished. I was a priest.

No human face could express such anguish, not the girl who sees her fiancé fall dead beside her nor the mother weeping by the empty cradle of her child, Eve sitting at the gate of paradise, the miser who finds a stone in place of his treasure, the poet who accidentally drops into the fire the only manuscript of his finest work: none of these could look more desperate or inconsolable. She turned as white as marble, her lovely arms fell down helpless by her sides, she leant against a pillar as if she would collapse in a faint. As for me, deathly pale and my brow bathed in sweat, I made my way towards the church door, staggering as I went, gasping for breath. The stone arches seemed to press down on my shoulders and I felt as if I was bearing the whole weight of the dome on my head.

As I was about to cross the threshold, a hand snatched mine, a women's hand. I had never touched one before. It was as cold as a snake and yet it left a mark as searing as a branding iron. It was she. 'Unhappy wretch, what have you done?' she said. Then she disappeared into the crowd.

On his way out of the church, the old bishop walked past me. His expression was solemn. I must have looked wild: now pale, now red, I was reeling with shock. One of my companions took pity on me and led me away for I would have been incapable, alone, of finding my own way back to the seminary. At a street corner, while the young priest accompanying me had his head averted for a moment, a black page in strange attire approached me and without pausing to speak handed me a little gold-rimmed purse, gesturing to me to hide it. I slipped it into my sleeve and left it there until I was alone in my cell. I opened the clasp and drew out a sheet of paper bearing the words: *Clarimonde, Concini Palace*. I was so unworldly I had never even heard of Clarimonde, in spite of her fame. I had no idea of the whereabouts of the Concini Palace. I made a thousand conjectures, each one wilder than the last, but to tell the truth, provided I could see her again, I was unconcerned as to whether she was a courtesan or a duchess.

The love which had just been born had taken root. It never occurred to me to pluck it out for that would have been impossible. Just one look at that woman had been enough: she held me in thrall! She had spoken and I no longer lived as my own man but in her and for her. I performed a thousand and one acts of folly, kissing my hand at the place where she had touched it and repeating her name for hours on end. I had only to close my eyes to see her as clearly as if she were there in the flesh and I repeated over and over again the words she had uttered at the church door: 'Unhappy wretch, what have you done?' I understood the full horror of the situation and the terrible sacrifices entailed by the vocation I had just embraced struck me with fearful clarity. To be a priest means to be chaste, never to love, never to make any distinctions of sex or age, to turn away from beauty, to become blind, to drag out one's life in a church or a cloister, to see only the dying, to keep vigil beside the bodies of strangers and to wear mourning for one's life with a black cassock for a shroud.

I felt the well-springs of life surge up inside me like a subterranean lake swelling and overflowing. My blood beat insistently in my veins and my youth, so long suppressed, burst out like the aloe that takes a hundred years to flower then explodes with the violence of a thunder clap.

How could I see Clarimonde again? I had no excuse for leaving the seminar as I had no friends in the town. I was not even destined to remain there, waiting, as I was, to hear which parish had been allotted me. I considered taking the bars away from the window but it was too high up and not having a ladder I dared not entertain the idea. Besides, I would only be able to get out at night. How could I negotiate that inextricable maze of streets? All these difficulties which would have been negligible for others were enormous for me, a poor young priest who had fallen in love yesterday and had no experience, no money, no clothes.

Had I not been a priest I could have seen her every day. I could have been her lover, her husband. Instead of wearing my wretched black shroud I could have had silk and velvet, gold chains, a sword and plumes like the handsome young chevaliers I had seen. My hair, instead of being cropped into a tonsure, could be falling to my neck in luxuriant curls. I would have a fine waxed moustache, I would be a man of fashion. But an hour spent kneeling at the altar, a few muttered words had forever cut me off from the land of the living and I knew that I had sealed my own tomb, bolted my own prison door. I went over to the window. The sky was a brilliant blue, the trees were dressed for spring. Nature mocked me, parading her joyful splendour. The square was full of people going about their business. Elegant young men and women made their way arm in arm towards the gardens and tree-lined avenues. Friends passed by in groups, singing on the way to the tavern. All that life and movement made me even more conscious of my state of mourning and solitude. A young mother sitting on a doorstep was playing with her child, kissing its little red mouth still empearled with drops of milk. She was cooing those sweet nothings that come naturally to mothers. The father smiled down on the pair, hugging his joy to his heart. I could not endure the sight of all these things. I closed the window and cast myself down on the bed with a terrible hatred and jealousy in my breast, gnawing at my fingers and the bed-clothes like a starving tiger.

I do not know how long I remained like this, but looking up, while in the grip of a terrible frenzy, I saw the abbé Serapion looking down at me. I was ashamed of myself, and bowing my head, covered my eyes with my hands.

'Romuald my friend, something extraordinary has happened to you', said Serapion after a few minutes' silence. 'Your conduct is quite inexplicable. You so calm and gentle, you so pious, are prowling about your cell like a wild beast. Take care, brother. Do not heed the devil's promptings. The Evil One is angry that you have dedicated yourself forever to the Lord and is stalking you like a ravening wolf. He is making one last effort to win you to him. My dear Romuald, make yourself a breastplate of prayer, a shield of self-mortification and fend off the enemy. You will conquer. Like gold, virtue must pass through the refiner's fire. Do not be afraid or discouraged; the most prudent souls have known such moments. Pray, fast, meditate. The Evil One will abandon the fight.

Serapion's words brought me back to my senses and I grew calmer. 'I came to tell you that you have been appointed priest at C***, after the death of the incumbent. The bishop has asked me to take you there. Be ready to leave tomorrow'. I nodded and the priest withdrew. I opened my missal and began to read, but the words grew blurred and I lost the thread. The book fell, unheeded, from my hands.

To leave tomorrow without seeing her again! Another obstacle added to those we already faced. To give up all hope of ever seeing her again. Write to her? Who would deliver the letter? Whom could I trust with such an errand, I, a man of God? Then, what Serapion had just told me about the tricks of the devil came back into my head. The strangeness of the incident, Clarimonde's unearthly beauty, the burning intensity of her eyes, the feverish touch of her hand, the confusion into which she had thrown me, the sudden change that had come over me, the instant obliteration of my religious fervour - all that proved conclusively the influence of the devil. That satin-skinned hand was probably the glove with which he covered his claws. These ideas filled me with dread, I picked up the missal that had rolled off my knee and returned to my prayers.

The next day, Serapion came to fetch me. Two mules loaded with our pitiful belongings stood waiting at the door. He took one and I the other. As we journeyed through the streets of the town I looked at all the windows and balconies to see if we could see Clarimonde but it was too early and the town had not yet opened its eyes. I tried to see behind the blinds and curtains of all the great houses we passed. Serapion attributed this curiosity of mine to admiration of the fine architecture, slowing the pace of his mount to give me a chance to look. At last we reached the town gate and began to climb the hill. When I was at the top I turned round to look once again at the place where Clarimonde lived. The town was overshadowed by a cloud. Its red and blue roofs merged in a uniformly neutral tint, surmounted, here and there by the smoke of early morning chimneys like white specks of foam. By a curious trick of the light a building which out-topped all the others draped in mist was silhouetted, pale gold in a solitary shaft of sunlight. The smallest details of the building could be seen clearly, the little towers, look-outs, casement windows and even the weather vanes.

'What is that place I see over there in the sunshine?' I enquired of Serapion. He shaded his eyes with his hand, looked and replied 'It is the old palace Prince Concini gave to the courtesan Clarimonde. Terrible things happen there'.

Just then, whether it was reality or illusion I cannot say, I thought I saw a slim white form glide across the terrace. It gleamed for a moment then vanished. It was Clarimonde!

Did she know that at that moment, from the high rough road that separated me from her, a road I was never to take again, I gazed long and ardently at the palace she lived in? A trick of the light seemed to bring it closer to me, as if to invite me to become its master. She must have known, for her soul was too close to mine not to feel its slightest stirring and it was the same feeling that impelled her, still in her night attire, to climb to the top of the terrace in the icy morning dew.

The cloud shadow reached the palace and now only a motionless sea of roofs and gables could be seen in the rising mist. Serapion urged on his mule, mine followed suit and a bend in the road hid from me for ever the town of S***, for I was never to return. After three days journey through unremarkable country, we saw through the trees the weather-cock of the church I was to administer. After following some winding streets lined with cottages and tiny walled gardens we found ourselves facing the church front which was not particularly impressive. There was a porch ornamented with some two or three coarsely chiselled pillars of sand stone and an arch, a tiled roof and buttresses of the same stone as the pillars. That was all. To the left was the cemetery, full of tall grasses with a great iron cross in the middle. To the right, in the shadow of the church, was the presbytery, a house of extreme simplicity and arid neatness. We entered: a few hens were pecking about on the ground outside. Accustomed no doubt to the black garb of clergymen, they showed no fear at our approach, hardly moving aside to let us pass. A hoarse bark was heard from within and an ancient dog ran up to greet us.

It was my predecessor's dog, dull of hair and eye, bearing all the tokens of extreme canine old age. I patted him gently and he trotted along beside me with an air of great satisfaction. An elderly woman who had been the housekeeper of the previous incumbent came out to meet us and after showing me into a low-ceilinged room, asked me if it was my intention to retain her services. I replied that I was happy to do so, together with the dog, the hens and all the furniture her master had left when he died, which caused her to go into transports of joy, the abbé Sérapion having given her on the spot the price she asked.

As soon as I was installed, Sérapion returned to the seminary. I was left alone and friendless. The thought of Clarimonde began again to obsess me and however hard I tried, I still could not drive that thought away. One evening as I walked along the box-edged paths of my little garden, I seemed to see through the surrounding hedge a woman's shape following my every movement, and the flash of two sea-green eyes through the leaves. It was only an illusion; when I crossed over, all I could find was a footprint in the sand, so small you would have taken it for a child's. The garden was surrounded by very high walls. I inspected all the corners and crevices but there was no one there. I could never explain it, any more than the other strange things that happened to me. I lived in this way for a year, fulfilling with care all the duties of my office, praying, fasting, preaching and visiting the sick, giving alms to the point of doing without necessities. But within me there was an abiding sterility and the well-springs of grace were denied me. I did not feel the happiness normally attendant on the fulfilment of a holy vocation. My thoughts were elsewhere and the words of Clarimonde came back to my lips like an involuntary refrain.... Think on this! For once looking upon a woman, for so venial a sin, I experienced for years the most distressing torment! My life was disrupted for ever.

I will not bore you with a description of all my inner defeats and victories, always followed by even greater defeats, I will only briefly mention one decisive occurrence. One night, there was a violent knocking on the door. The old housekeeper went to see what it was and a man of dark complexion and rich outlandish garb, armed with a long dagger, was revealed by the light of Barbara's lantern. Her first reaction was one of fear but the man reassured her, saying that he must see me at once on a matter concerning my ministry. Barbara admitted him to my room. I was about to retire to bed. The man told me that his mistress, a very great lady, was on the point of death and had asked for a priest. I said I would go with him. Taking with me everything necessary for the sacrament of extreme unction, I hurried downstairs. At the door, two horses black as night were pawing the ground impatiently and snorting fire. The man held the bridle and helped me to mount one of the horses, then jumped up on to the other, merely by resting his hand lightly on the pommel and pressing the horse's flanks with his knees, he loosed the reins and the horse set off like an arrow from a bow. He was holding the bridle of my horse which also set off at a gallop and remained perfectly in step with the other. We kept up a scorching pace, the earth grey beneath us and the black silhouettes of the trees flying past like an army in full retreat. We passed through a forest so cold and dark that I felt a shiver of superstitious terror. The sparks struck on the road by our horses' hooves left a trail of fire and if anyone had seen us at that time of night he would have taken us for two spectres riding in a nightmare. Will-o-the-wisps crossed our path from time to time and night owls hooted from the depths of the wood where, here and there the phosphorescent eyes of wild-cats pierced the gloom. The horses' manes tangled wildly in the wind, sweat poured down their flanks and their panting breath burst noisily from their lungs. But when he felt them flagging the horseman uttered a harsh, scarcely human cry to spur them on and the break-neck charge began again with redoubled frenzy. At last that headlong flight came to a stop. A great dark building dotted here and there with brilliant spots of light loomed over us. The ring of our horses' hooves struck loud on the paving of the forecourt and we entered by way of a cavernous opening between two enormous towers. The chateau was alive with hectic activity. Servants bearing flaming torches crossed and recrossed the central courtyard, lights could be seen moving up and down between the floors. I saw a confusion of great structures, columns, arcades, flights of steps, ramps, a fairy-tale extravagance of architecture.

A black page, the same one who had given me Clarimonde's note, came forward to help me dismount and a majordomo in black velvet with a gold chain about his neck and an ivory cane in his hand, led the way. Tears ran down his cheeks on to his white beard. 'Too late', he said, shaking his head, 'too late, my lord priest. But if you could not save the soul, come and keep vigil over the poor lifeless body'. He took me by the arm and led me to the funeral chamber. I was weeping as much as he was for I realised that the dead woman was none other than my beloved Clarimonde. A prie-Dieu had been placed next to the bed. A blue flame flickering in a bronze dish cast a pale uncertain light over the room and revealed the vague outline of some projecting cornice or piece of furniture. On the table a faded white rose in a finely-chiselled urn had dropped all its petals save one; they lay at the base of the vase like sweet-smelling tears. A broken black domino mask, a fan, disguises of all kinds, lay about on armchairs and suggested that the dead woman had arrived unexpectedly in this sumptuous abode. I knelt down without daring to look at the bed and began to recite the psalms with great fervour, thanking God that He had put the tomb between the thought of that woman and myself, so that I could add her name, now cleared of sin, to my prayers. But gradually my ardour diminished and I fell into a state of reverie. That room bore no resemblance to a room of death. Instead of the fetid, corpse-tainted air I was accustomed to breathe at such times, a dreamy perfume of oriental essences, a bewitchingly feminine fragrance wafted gently in the warm atmosphere. The pale half-light resembled the twilight of a room destined for amorous delights rather than the yellow-shaded candle flame that burns next to the dead. I pondered the strange coincidence that had given me back Clarimonde at the very moment I was to lose her for ever and a sigh of regret escaped my breast. I had the impression that there was an echoing sigh behind me and I turned involuntarily. As I turned, my glance rested on the bed I had until then avoided. The red damask curtains embroidered with flowers held back by twisted cords of gold revealed the dead woman lying full length, her hands folded on her breast. She was covered in a veil of dazzling whiteness, intensified by the deep scarlet of the hangings, so fine that it concealed nothing of the graceful shape of her body, revealing those beautiful curves, like the neck of a swan, that death itself could not freeze into rigidity. She was like an alabaster figure sculpted by a consummate artist or a sleeping girl on whom snow had fallen.

My senses were reeling, overwhelmed by the perfume of that alcove. The intoxicating perfume of the faded rose went to my head and I paced restlessly round the room, stopping again and again to contemplate the lovely corpse beneath its transparent shroud. Strange thoughts assailed me. I imagined she was not really dead, that this was merely a ruse to attract me to her chateau and tell me about her love for me. For a moment I even thought I saw a movement of her feet beneath the whiteness of the veil, disturbing the folds of the shroud.

Then I said to myself: 'Is that really Clarimonde? What proof have I? Could not that page have passed into the service of another woman? I am mad to grieve and upset myself in this way'. But my heart told me: 'It is indeed she'. I approached the bed and stared attentively at the object of my uncertainty. Shall I admit it? That perfection of form, purified and sanctified by the shadow of death disturbed my senses more than was natural. That repose was so like sleep one might have been deceived into believing it was sleep. I forgot I had come there to perform the office of the dead and I imagined I was a young husband entering the room of his bride who hid her face for modesty and would not show herself to him. At once grief-stricken and mad with delight, quivering with fear mingled with pleasure I leaned towards her and took in my hand a corner of the sheet. I raised it slowly holding my breath for fear of waking her. The blood beat so hard in my veins my head was ringing with it and my brow ran with sweat as if I had raised a marble slab. It was the Clarimonde I had seen at the church at the time of my ordination. She was just as beautiful: death had simply added another dimension to her beauty. The pallor of her cheeks and the subdued rose of her lips, her long eyelashes tracing their dark fringe on that whiteness lent her an air of melancholy purity and refined suffering which exerted an intense power of seduction. Her long, loose-flowing hair with which a few little blue flowers were intermingled made a pillow for her head, and covered her bare shoulders with their tumbling curls. Her beautiful hands, purer and more transparent than consecrated bread, were crossed in an attitude of tranquil piety and prayer, attenuating the sensuality that even in death was expressed in the exquisite perfection of bare arms still wearing their pearl bracelets. I stood for some time gazing down in mute adoration and the more I looked the less I could believe that life had for ever deserted that lovely body. I cannot say if it was an illusion or the glow of the lamp but it seemed as if the blood began again to flow beneath that smooth pallor. She remained, however, perfectly still. I touched her arm lightly: it was cold, but no colder than her hand that day it had brushed mine at the church door. I sat down again, bending towards her face and shedding the warm dew of my tears on her cheeks. Such bitter despair and impotence! How painful was that vigil! I would have loved to gather all my life into a ball and give it to her, to reanimate her with the flame consuming me. Night was coming on. Feeling the approach of that moment of eternal separation, I could not resist the urge to imprint with a kiss the dead lips of the one who had been my only love. A faint breath mingled miraculously with mine and Clarimonde's lips responded. Her eyes opened and seemed to brighten, she sighed, and uncrossing her arms she put them round my neck. 'At last, Romuald', she said in a voice like the dying echoes of a harp. 'What are you doing here? I have waited so long for you I have died of waiting. But now we are betrothed I will be able to see you and come to you. Farewell, Romuald! I love you; that is all I wished to say and I return to you the life you brought back to me with your kiss. A bientôt!'

Her head fell back but her arms remained round

my neck as if to hold me prisoner. A gust of wind blew open the window and entered the room. The last petal of the white rose trembled for a moment like a wing on the end of its stem then detached itself and flew through the open window bearing with it the soul of Clarimonde. The lamp went out and I fell down in a faint over the lovely corpse.

When I came to, I was lying on my bed in my little room at the presbytery whilst the old dog licked my hand. Barbara bustled about the room, opening and closing drawers or stirring medicinal potions in glasses. When she saw me open my eyes, the old women uttered a cry of joy, the dog barked and wagged its tail; but I was so weak I could not utter a single word or make the slightest movement. I heard since that I had spent three days in that condition, giving no other sign of life than my barely perceptible breathing. Those three days were a blank in my life; I do not know where my spirit wandered all that time.

I can remember nothing. Barbara told me that the same dark-skinned man who had come to fetch me brought me back home in the morning in a closed carriage and left immediately. As soon as I could collect my thoughts I went over in my mind all the events of that fateful night. First I thought I had been the victim of some magic illusion but indications of all too real a nature soon destroyed that supposition. I could not believe I had been dreaming when Barbara had seen the man with the two black horses just as I had and could describe precisely their trappings and accoutrements. And yet no one in the district could identify a chateau like the one where I had found Clarimonde again.

One morning the abbé Serapion entered my room. Barbara had told him I was ill and he hastened to visit me. Although his visit proved the affectionate interest he took in my welfare, it did not cause me as much pleasure as it ought to have done. Serapion's eyes expressed a penetrating curiosity which disturbed me. He made me feel embarrassed and guilty. He had been the first to become aware of my spiritual confusion and I resented it.

As he made enquiries about my health in a hypocritically honeyed tone, he stared at me with his tawny eyes and probed about in my soul. Then he asked me a few questions about how I was getting on with my parochial duties, if I was happy, how I spent my time when I was not working, if I had made any friends among the local people, which books I preferred to read and a hundred and one other matters. I answered as briefly as possible and without waiting for me to finish, he himself moved on to other things. It was obvious that this conversation had no connection with what he really wanted to say to me. Then, without any warning, and as if it were a piece of news he had just that moment recalled and was afraid of forgetting, he said in a clear and penetrating voice which sounded in my ear like the last trump:

'Clarimonde the fabled courtesan died recently after an orgy which lasted seven days and seven nights. The abominations of the orgies of Cleopatra and Balthazar were recreated, in a feast of infernal splendour. What an age we live in! The guests were served by dusky slaves speaking an unknown tongue; perhaps they were demons from hell. The least of them wore garments so rich they could have graced an emperor. There have always been very strange stories about Clarimonde and all her lovers have met a wretched or violent death. It has been said she was a ghoul or a vampire but I believe she was the devil himself'.

He fell silent, observing me more attentively than before to see the effect of his words on me. I could not help starting when Clarimonde's name was mentioned and the news of her death, apart from the pain it caused me by its curious coincidence with the nocturnal scene I had witnessed, threw me into a state of confusion and alarm which showed clearly on my face however hard I tried to conceal it. Serapion threw me a glance of anxious severity, He said: 'My son, I must warn you, you are on the brink of an abyss. Take care you do not fall in. Satan's claws are long and tombs do not always keep their dead.

'Clarimonde's tomb should be sealed with a triple seal. From what I hear, it is not the first time she has died. May God be with you, Romuald'.

With these words, Serapion walked slowly to the door. I did not see him again, for he left almost at once for S***.

I was completely recovered and had resumed my normal employment. The memory of Clarimonde and the words of the good abbé were always foremost in my mind but no extraordinary event had occurred to fulfil the fearful predictions of Serapion and I was beginning to believe that my apprehensions and terrors were exaggerated.

But one night I had a dream. I had scarcely fallen asleep when I heard a clatter of curtain rings as the draperies round my bed were pulled apart. I raised myself up on one elbow and saw the shadow of a woman. I at once recognised Clarimonde. She was carrying a little lamp like the sort customarily found in tombs. Its light lent a pink transparency to her tapering fingers that gradually shaded into the opaque milky whiteness of her bare arm. Her only garment was the linen shroud which had covered her on her death-bed, and she held the folds closely to her as if she were ashamed to be wearing so little but her little hand was not equal to the task. She was so white that the colour of the drapery merged with her flesh beneath the lamp's pale gleam. Wrapped in the flimsy material which showed all the curves of her body, she was more like the marble statue of a *baigneuse* than a creature of flesh and blood. Dead or alive, statue or woman, wraith or living being, her beauty had not changed. Only the green blaze of her eyes was slightly dimmed and her mouth, once so red, was now faintly coloured like the pale rose of her cheeks. The little blue flowers

I had seen in her hair were quite dry and had lost almost all their petals. None of this in any way detracted from her charm which was so great that in spite of the singularity of the occurrence and the inexplicable way she had entered the room I did not for an instant feel afraid.

She set the lamp down on the table and sat at the foot of my bed then, leaning towards me and speaking in a silvery caressing tone of voice I never heard before or since, she said: 'I have been a long time, dear Romuald, and you must have thought I had forgotten you. But I come from a very distant land, a land from which no one else has yet returned. There is neither night nor day in the land I come from, only space and shadow. There is neither road nor pathway, no earth for the feet nor air for the wing. But here I am, because love is stronger than death and will conquer it in the end. I have seen such unhappy faces, such dreadful things on my journey! How hard it was for my soul to find its body again and enter it after willing myself back to this world. What a struggle to raise the stone with which I was covered! See! The palms of my hands are all bruised with it! Kiss them to make them better, my love'. She placed her cold hands on my mouth and I kissed them many times over while she looked at me with a smile of unspeakable delight.

I admit, to my shame, that I had completely forgotten the words of the abbé Serapion and my priestly state. I had yielded unresisting, at the first onslaught. I had not even tried to resist: the coolness of Clarimonde's skin pervaded mine and I shuddered pleasurably. Poor child! In spite of everything, it was hard to believe she was a demon. She could not have looked less like one, for never had Satan more cleverly concealed his claws and his horns! She was reclining at the foot of the bed in a pose of nonchalant coquetry. She ran her fingers through my hair from time to time, twisting it into curls as if she were trying out new ways of dressing it. I abandoned myself totally to her caresses as she prattled away beguilingly. Strangely enough, I felt no surprise. On the contrary, it seemed the most natural thing in all the world.

'I loved you long before I ever saw you, dear Romuald, and I searched everywhere for you. You were my ideal and when I saw you in church at that fatal moment I knew I had found you. I looked at you with all the love I felt and will always feel for you. It was a look that would have sent a cardinal to his damnation and made a king kneel down at my feet in the midst of his court. You remained unmoved and preferred your God.

'How I envy God, for you loved and still love Him more than me!

'Unhappy that I am! Never will your heart be mine alone though you brought me back to life with a kiss, I the dead Clarimonde who for you have forced the gates of death and offer you now a life I regained only to make you happy!'

Her words were punctuated with delirious caresses which distracted my senses and my reason to the point where I did not fear to utter a terrible blasphemy: to console her, I told her I loved her as much as I loved God.

Her eyes rekindled and shone like emeralds. 'Truly? As much as God'? she cried, embracing me. 'In that case, you will come with me, you will follow me wherever I go. You will discard your ugly black clothes. You will be the proudest and the most envied of knights, you will be my lover. To be the lover of Clarimonde who refused a pope, think of that! What a happy golden life will be ours! When do we leave, sir knight?'

'Tomorrow!' I cried in my rapture.

'Tomorrow then'! she echoed. 'I will have time to change my clothes, for these are somewhat scanty and useless for travel. I must also instruct my servants who believe me to be well and truly dead and are in deep mourning for me. Money, clothes, carriages, all will be ready. I will call for you tomorrow at the same hour. Farewell, dear heart'! She lightly touched my brow with her lips. The lamp went out, the curtains closed, I saw nothing more. A sleep, dreamless and deep, came over me and lasted until morning. I woke later than usual and the memory of my astonishing vision tormented me all day. In the end, I concluded it was a figment of my imagination. And yet the impressions had been so strong it was hard indeed to believe they were not real. It was not without apprehension that I retired to bed after praying that God would take from me all evil thoughts and protect the chastity of my sleep.

I quickly fell asleep and my dream continued. The curtains parted. Clarimonde appeared, but not the pale Clarimonde in her white shroud, the violet of death upon her cheeks. This was a creature exuding cheerful vivacity, superbly dressed in a travelling costume of green velvet embroidered with gold, an underskirt of satin revealed at the sides by the turned-back hem. Her blonde hair tumbled down in heavy curls from beneath a wide-brimmed black felt hat trimmed with white ostrich feathers. In her hand she held a little riding whip tipped with a golden whistle. She tapped me lightly with it and said: 'So this is how you prepare for our departure, handsome sleeper! I expected to find you up and about. Get up quickly; we have no time to lose'. I jumped down from the bed.

'Now get dressed and let us be off' said she, pointing to a small parcel she had brought. 'The horses are restless. We should be ten miles away already'.

I dressed hurriedly as she handed me each garment in turn, laughing at my clumsiness and guiding me when I went wrong. She combed my hair into shape and when she had finished held out to me a little pocket mirror of Venetian glass framed in silver filigree, saying: 'There now. Would you like to engage me as your valet de chambre?'

I did not recognise myself, so great was the

change. I as little resembled my old self as a statue resembles a block of stone. My old face had been but a crude outline of the new one I saw in the mirror. I was handsome and my vanity was flattered by the metamorphosis. These elegant clothes, this richly embroidered coat had turned me into an entirely different person and I marvelled at the transforming power of a few yards of cloth cut in a certain way. My new appearance affected me so much that after only ten minutes I became quite conceited.

To get used to my new self I took a few turns about the room. Clarimonde gazed at me with a look of maternal pride and seemed delighted with her hard work. Then she exclaimed: 'That will do, my dear Romuald. Let us be off. We have a long way to go and at this rate we will never get there'. Doors sprang open before her as soon as she touched them and we passed the dog without waking him.

At the door we found Margheritone, the equerry who had attended me before. He held by the bridle three black horses which must have been Spanish jennets born of mares serviced by the wind for they galloped as fast and the moon which had risen to light our way spun like a cartwheel in the sky. We could see it jumping from tree to tree on our right, panting to keep up with us. We soon arrived at a plain where a carriage awaited us beside a thicket, harnessed to four mighty horses. We mounted and the postilions spurred them on into a headlong gallop. I had one arm round Clarimonde's waist and one of her hands in mine. She leant her head against my shoulder. Never had I felt such happiness. In that moment I forgot everything else. It no more crossed my mind that I was a priest then I remembered being in my mother's womb, so great was the Evil One's power over me. From that moment on, my personality underwent a kind of reduplication which turned me into two different men, neither of whom knew the other. Sometimes I thought I was a priest who dreamed each night he was a nobleman and some times a nobleman who thought he was a priest.

I could no longer distinguish dream from reality; I had no idea where the one began and the other ended. The vain young libertine mocked the priest and the priest hated the dissolute life of the young seigneur. Two spirals twisting round each other without touching illustrate perfectly the two-headed life I was leading, but in spite of the unnatural character of the situation, I never once came near to madness. I always clearly distinguished between my two lives. There was only one thing I could not understand: it was that an awareness of the same self could exist in two so very different men. It was an anomaly I could not understand, whether I believed myself to be the priest of the little village of C*** or *il signor Romualdo*, acknowledged lover of Clarimonde.

In any case, I was, or believed I was, in Venice. I could not yet separate illusion from reality in this strange adventure. We lived in a great marble palace on the Grand Canal, full of frescos and statues with two Titians of the master's finest period in Clarimonde's bedroom. It was a palace fit for a king. We each had our gondolier, our music room and our poet. Clarimonde led the life of a queen; she had something of Cleopatra in her nature. I in my turn lived like a prince's son and I strutted about as if I were the highest in the land. I would not have stood aside to let the doge himself go by and since Satan fell down from heaven, there cannot have been anyone more proud or more insolent.

I frequented the Casino and played for high stakes. I was acquainted with the cream of society - sons of ruined families, actresses, crooks, parasites and ruffians. But in spite of this life of debauchery I remained faithful to Clarimonde. I loved her to distraction. She had the power endlessly to refuel the fires of love; to be unfaithful to her was an impossibility, for she was twenty mistresses in one, she was so changeable and assumed so many disguises she was all womankind, a veritable chameleon. With her you committed the act of infidelity you would have committed with other women, assuming at will the character, type and appearance of whichever woman happened to appeal to you. She returned my love a hundred-fold and it was in vain that all the young nobles and even the elders of the secret Tribunal of Ten offered her wealth and position unparalleled. A Foscari asked for her hand in marriage and she refused. She had enough gold and wanted only love, a young pure love she had awakened herself and which would be the first and the last. I would have been perfectly happy were it not for an accursed nightmare which returned every night in which I imagined I was a village priest doing penance for my daytime excesses! Reassured by my everyday life with her, I hardly ever thought of the extraordinary way in which I had made her acquaintance. All the same, what the abbé had told me sometimes came back to me and made me uneasy. For some time, Clarimonde's health had not been good. Her complexion became daily more deathly pale. Doctors who attended her knew nothing about her condition and hardly knew what to do. They prescribed a few harmless medicines and never returned. But every day her colour faded and she grew colder. She was almost as white and as dead as on that memorable night in the unknown chateau. I was desolate to see her wasting away. Touched by my grief, she smiled sweetly and sadly with the smile of resignation of those who know they are going to die.

One morning I was sitting by her bed, breakfasting from a little table so as not to leave her for a minute when, in the act of cutting a piece of fruit I accidentally made a deep gash in my finger. The blood spurted out in scarlet jets of which a few drops fell on Clarimonde. Her eyes lit up, her face took on an expression of fierce wild joy I had never seen before. She jumped down from off the bed with animal agility, the agility of a monkey or a cat, fastened on to my wound and began to suck it with an expression of unspeakable delight, She took tiny sips of the blood, slowly and reverently, like a gourmet savouring a wine from Xeres or Syracuse. She half closed her green eyes and the pupils became slit-like instead of round. From time to time she stopped to kiss my hand before beginning again to press her lips to the mouth of the wound to extract from it a few more drops of red. When she saw that the blood had stopped flowing she looked up with a new light in her eyes, her face restored to its fullness, rose-coloured like a May morning, her hands warm and soft, more beautiful than ever and in perfect health.

'I am not going to die!' she cried, her arms round my neck, in a state of joy bordering on hysteria. 'I can go on loving you for a long time. My life lies within yours and all that is mine comes from you. A few drops of your noble rich blood, more precious than all the elixirs in the world, have given me back my life'.

This scene haunted me and inspired me with

strange doubts as regards Clarimonde and that night, when sleep took me back to my presbytery, I found the abbé more serious and careworn than ever. He looked steadily at me and said: 'Not content with losing your soul, you now wish to lose your body. Unfortunate young man, what a trap you have fallen into!' The tone of voice in which he uttered these words impressed me deeply, but in spite of its intensity the impression soon faded and a myriad new preoccupations drove it out if my mind. One evening, however, I saw in my mirror, whose treacherous angle had not been realised by Clarimonde, that she was dropping some powder in the cup of spiced wine she always prepared for me after meals. I took the cup, pretended to drink then placed it on the table as if to finish it later at my leisure. Taking advantage of a moment when she had her back turned, I threw the contents away under the table. I then returned to my room and lay down, determined not to sleep so as to see what would happen. I did not wait long. Clarimonde entered in her night attire. Unveiling herself, she lay down beside me. When she was sure I was asleep, she uncovered my arm and drew a gold pin from her hair. Then she began to murmur in a low voice: 'A drop, only one little red drop, a ruby on the point of my needle!... As you still love me, I must not die ... Poor love! Your beautiful blood, so scarlet red, I must drink it. Sleep, my only one; sleep, my god, my child; I will do you no harm, I will only take as much of your life as will sustain mine. If I did not love you so well I could have loved others whose veins I would exhaust; but since I have known you everyone but you is hateful to me... Ah, lovely arm! How round, how white! I will never dare pierce that pretty blue vein! As she spoke, she wept and I felt her tears on my arm. At last she made up her mind, pricked me with her needle and began to suck the blood. Although she had scarcely drunk a few drops for fear of exhausting me, she wrapped a little bandage round the arm after rubbing the wound with an ointment which healed it at once.

I could have no more doubts. Abbé Serapion was right. But in spite of my certainty, I could not help loving Clarimonde and I would willingly have given her all the blood she needed to sustain her false existence. Besides, I was not much afraid, for the woman was answerable for the vampire and what I had heard and seen reassured me entirely. I had at that time youthful veins which would not readily be drained and I was not trading my life in drops of blood. I would willingly have opened the arm myself and said: 'Drink! And may my love enter your body with my blood'. I avoided any mention of the drug she had prepared for me or the scene with the needle and we lived in the most perfect harmony. But my priestly scruples tormented me more than ever and I was at a loss to find new ways of mortifying my flesh. Although all my visions were involuntary and unprovoked I did not dare to touch the blessed sacrament with such sinful hands and a spirit sullied by such debauchery, real or imagined. To prevent falling into these tiring hallucinations I tried to stay awake, I held my eyelids open with my fingers and I remained standing against the wall, struggling with all my might and main against sleep. But soon the sands of weariness entered my eyes and seeing that it was vain to struggle, I let fall my arms from discouragement and weariness and was dragged again by the current into perfidious waters. Serapion exhorted me vehemently and reproached me with my pitiful lack of spiritual fibre. One day when I had been more than usually tormented, he said: 'To get rid of this obsession there is only one course of action. Although it is extreme, it must be tried. Great ills need great remedies. I know where Clarimonde is buried. We must exhume her so you can see how pitiful is the state of your loved one. You will not be tempted then to lose your immortal soul for a putrid corpse eaten up by worms and on the brink of disintegration. You will come back to your senses, don't doubt it'. As for me, I was so weary of my double life that I agreed. Determined to know once and for all which of the two, priest or nobleman, was prey to an illusion, I made up my mind to kill one of the two living inside me to the advantage of the other or else to kill them both, for such a life could no longer continue. Abbé Serapion provided himself with a pickaxe, a lever and a lantern and at midnight we made our way towards the cemetery with whose lay-out he was perfectly familiar. After holding the lantern up to the inscriptions on several tombs we arrived at last at a stone half hidden in the tall grass and eaten away by moss and ivy. We deciphered these few lines of an inscription:

Here lies Clarimonde
Who in her lifetime
Was the most beautiful woman in the world

'This is the place', said Serapion, and putting down his lantern, he slid the lever into a crack beneath the stone, and began to raise it up. The stone yielded and he began work with the pickaxe. I watched him at work, my mood blacker and more silent than the night itself. As for him, bent over his task, sweat poured from his brow and he breathed painfully like a dying man. It was a strange sight: whoever had seen us would have taken us for profane grave-robbers rather than men of God. Serapion's zeal had something hard and wild about it making him more like a demon than an apostle or an angel. His face, with its austere features hollowed deeply by the rays of the lantern did nothing to reassure me. I broke out all over in a cold sweat and my hair seemed to stand on end. Deep inside me I regarded Serapion's course of action as an abominable sacrilege and I wished that from the dark clouds rolling heavily overhead would come forked lightning to reduce him to ashes. The owls perched among the cypress trees, disturbed by the bright lantern flapped their wings against its glass sides with plaintive cries. Foxes yelped in the distance; a thousand sinister noises broke the silence. At last, Serapion's axe struck the coffin whose boards resounded with that terrible dull thud with which lifeless things respond when they are disturbed. He lifted up the lid and I saw Clarimonde as white as marble, her hands joined, as if in prayer. The white shroud covered her from head to foot. A little drop of red gleamed like a rose at the corner of her colourless lips. At this sight, Serapion flew into a rage: 'So there you are, you demon, you shameless courtesan, drinker of gold and blood!' He sprinkled with holy water the body and the coffin on which he traced the sign of the cross. Poor Clarimonde had scarcely been touched by that holy dew than her lovely body crumbled into dust. It became a hideous shapeless mass of ash and semi-calcined bones. 'Behold your mistress', said the inexorable priest, indicating the pitiful remains. 'Are you still tempted to stroll arm in arm with your belle at the Lido or at Fusina, Seigneur Romuald?' I went back to my presbytery and the Seigneur Romuald, lover of Clarimonde, detached himself from the poor priest with whom he had so long kept such strange company. And yet, the next night, I saw Clarimonde again. She said, as she had that first time at the church door: 'Unhappy wretch! What have you done? Why did you heed that imbecile priest? What have I done to you that you should violate my poor tomb and reveal the pitiful sight of my disintegration? All communication between our souls and bodies is now broken for ever. Farewell. You will miss me' She vanished into thin air like smoke and I never saw her again.

Alas, she spoke truly. I have more than once missed her; I still miss her. The peace of my soul has been dearly bought. The love of God was scarcely enough to replace hers... And that, my friend, is the story of my youth. Never look at a woman; walk with your eyes to the ground, for however chaste and serene you are, it is only a minute's work to lose your soul for all Eternity.

THE MUMMY'S FOOT
by Théophile Gautier
First published in *Le Musée des Familles*
1840

THE MUMMY'S FOOT

I wandered idly into one of those curiosity shops where they sell what is called bric à brac in that Parisian argot mostly unintelligible to the rest of France.

No doubt you have looked through the windows of one of those shops which are so numerous now that it has become fashionable to buy antique furniture and every stockbroker has his 'mediaeval room'. They are a combination of scrap merchants' yards, upholsterers' workshops, alchemists' laboratories and painters' studios. In their mysterious caverns, where the blinds let in a prudent half-light, the most ancient substance of all is dust. The spiders' webs are more authentic than the old lace and the antique fruit-wood is younger than the mahogany just arrived from America.

The shop of my bric à brac seller was a veritable Aladdin's cave. Every century and every country was represented. An Etruscan terra-cotta lamp sat on a Boulle cabinet with ebony panels chastely striped in bronze. A Louis XV chaise longue nonchalantly extended its cabriole legs beneath a massive Louis XIII oak table, heavily decorated with scrolls and carvings of leaves and imps.

The banded curve of the breastplate of a suit of armour from Milan gleamed in one corner. Cupids and nymphs in biscuit porcelain, grotesque figurines from China, pale green celadon crackle-glazed vases, Saxony and old Sèvres cups littered the shelves and corner cupboards.

Enormous Japanese plates with red and blue designs picked out in gold sat resplendent on the shelves of dressers alongside Bernard Palissy enamels with vipers, frogs and lizards in relief.

Cascades of silver-threaded organza, floods of brocade sparkling with innumerable gold dots in a slanting sunbeam poured out of a cupboard, portraits of all periods of history smiled through their yellowing varnish in their faded frames.

The shopkeeper followed me carefully round the tortuous passage between the piles of furniture, smoothing down with his hand the dangerous tails of my coat, observing my elbows with the anxious gaze of the antiques dealer and the money lender.

He had a curious face: an enormous skull, as shiny as a knee, surrounded by a fine halo of white hair that emphasised the salmon pink of his skin, giving him a misleading air of patriarchal bonhomie. This impression was corrected by the gleam of two little yellow eyes blinking in their sockets like a couple of gold louis on mercury. The nose was aquiline, of levantine cast. His slender hands with their prominent sinews were like the strings of a violin, the claw-like nails that resembled the tips of a bat's wing fluttered about in senile agitation, disturbing to behold. But those constantly-twitching hands grew steadier than steel tongs or lobsters' claws the minute they picked up some precious object, an onyx goblet, a piece of Venetian glass or a Bohemian crystal dish. The funny old man was so rabbinical-looking he would have been burnt on sight three centuries ago.

'Won't you buy anything today, monsieur? Just look at this Malayan kris. Its blade is as sinuous as a flame. See the grooves to channel the blood and the reverse serration for disembowelling the victim when you pull it out! It is a formidable weapon of exceptional quality and would be just right in your collection... This two-handed sword is very fine, made by Joseph de la Hera, and this heavy sword with a pierced hand-guard - what a superb piece of work!'

'No; I have quite enough weapons and instruments of death. I would like a figurine, some kind of object I can use as a paper-weight. I can't bear all those cheap brass things they sell at the stationer's, the sort you find on everybody's desk'.

Ferreting about among his bygones, the old gnome produced bits of antique, or so-called antique bronze, pieces of malachite, small Hindu or Chinese idols, jade buddhas, the incarnation of Brahma or Vishnu, remarkably suitable for the secular purpose of keeping papers and letters in their place.

I was hesitating between a porcelain dragon covered in warts, its maw adorned with tusks and whiskers and a little Mexican fetish of revolting appearance depicting the god Witziliputzili in the nude when I noticed a charming foot that I took at first for a fragment from some ancient statue of Venus.

It had those lovely tawny russet shades which give Florentine bronze its warmth and vivacity, so much more appealing than the green patina of ordinary bronzes which look like statues in a state of decay. Its rounded contours, polished by twenty centuries of amorous kisses, gleamed with the sheen of satin. It must be a Corinthian bronze, from the best period, perhaps even a casting by Lysippe!

'I'll take this foot', I said to the merchant who gave me a sly sardonic look as he held out the object for my inspection.

I was surprised at how light it was. It was not a metal foot but a foot of flesh, an embalmed foot. Looking closely, you could see the grain of the skin and the almost imperceptible imprint of the winding sheet. The toes were slender and delicate, ending in perfect nails, pure and transparent as agate. The great toe, drawn away from the others in the antique style gave it the unconstrained look of a bird's foot. The arch, scarcely marked by a few near-invisible lines, showed it had never been in contact with earth but only with the finest of rush matting from the Nile and the most sumptuous of panther skins.

'Aha! so you want the foot of Princess Hermonthis', said the merchant with a curious little laugh, staring at me with his owl's eyes. "For a paper weight! What an original idea, an artistic idea! If anyone had told the old Pharaoh that the foot of his beloved daughter would be used as a paper weight he would have been very surprised especially as he had a mountain of granite hollowed out for her triple coffin, painted and gilded, covered in hieroglypics with fine pictures of the last judgment' he added in a low voice, as if he were talking to himself.

'How much do you want for this mummy fragment?'

'As much as I can get; it's a superb piece. If I had the other one you would not get away with less than five hundred francs. Nothing is rarer than a Pharaoh's daughter'.

'Obviously it is out of the ordinary, but how much do you want? I warn you I only have five louis on me. I will buy anything costing five louis, no more'.

'Five louis for the foot of Princess Hermonthis! That's very little, very little, an authentic foot', said the dealer shaking his head and rolling his eyeballs.

'Never mind. Take it and I'll let you have something to wrap it in as well', he added. rolling it up in an old scrap of damask. 'Very fine, real damask, Indian damask, single dyed. It's strong but soft' he muttered, fingering the threadbare cloth out of a long-standing habit of the trade that made him praise an object of so little value to him he was prepared to give it away.

He dropped the gold coins into a sort of mediaeval pouch hanging from his belt, repeating over to himself: 'The foot of Princess Hermonthis used as a paper weight!'

Then turning to stare at me with eyeballs glowing redly he said in a voice as harsh as the howl of a cat that has just swallowed a fishbone:

'The old Pharaoh won't be pleased; he loved his daughter, the dear man'.

'You speak of him as if you were his contemporary. You may be old, but you hardly go back to the time of the pyramids', I said with a laugh from the shop doorway.

I went home delighted with my new acquisition.

I immediately made use of it, placing the foot of the divine Princess Hermonthis on a pile of papers, rough copies of some verses, an indecipherable tissue of crossings-out, unfinished articles, forgotten letters posted in a drawer, a failing of absent-minded people. The effect was charming, bizarre, romantic.

Highly satisfied with the embellishment, I went

out for a walk with a feeling of self-importance and pride befitting a man who has the inestimable advantage over everybody else of possessing a piece of the Princess Hermonthis, the Pharaoh's daughter.

I considered to be supremely ridiculous all those who did not possess, as I did, such a famously Egyptian paperweight. The true vocation of a man of sense seemed to be to own a mummy's foot to put on his desk.

Fortunately, I happened to meet some friends, which distracted me from my besotted obsession with my new acquisition. I had dinner with them as it would have been difficult for me to have dinner with myself, in such a frame of mind.

When I returned later that night, a trifle intoxicated, a faint whiff of oriental perfume gently tickled my olfactory organ; the warmth of the room had heated the natrum, bitumen and myrrh with which the embalmers had saturated the body of the princess. It was a suave but penetrating perfume; four thousand years had not effaced it.

The ancient Egyptians dreamed of eternity; their perfumes have the solidity of granite and last as long.

Soon I was drinking deep from the black cup of sleep. For an hour or two everything was swallowed up in the amorphous darkness of oblivion.

Then the darkness in my brain began to lift and dreams brushed over me on silent wing.

The eyes of my soul were opened and I saw my room as it really was. I might have thought I was awake but I was vaguely aware that I was sleeping and something strange was about to happen.

The scent of myrrh had become stronger and I had a slight headache which I attributed quite reasonably to the few glasses of champagne we had drunk to the unknown gods and to our future success.

I looked round my room with a feeling of expectancy nothing seemed to justify. The furniture was in its proper place, the lamp was burning on the console table, softly shaded by the milky whiteness of its opaque crystal shade. The water colours gleamed beneath their Bohemian glass, the curtains hung down langorously; everything was peacefully at rest.

A few moments later, however, the quiet of my room seemed disturbed, the woodwork creaked faintly, the log buried under the dying embers suddenly threw out a spurt of blue gas and the round supports for the coat hooks seemed like metal eyes watching out, as I was, to see what was going to happen.

My gaze rested on the table on which I had placed the foot of Princess Hermonthis.

Instead of standing still as befits a foot embalmed for four thousand years, it was jumping agitatedly about on the papers like an alarmed frog. It might have been in contact with an electric charge. I distinctly heard the tap of its little heel, like a gazelle's hoof.

I began to feel some dissatisfaction regarding my acquisition, preferring sedentary paperweights and thinking it unnatural to see feet walking about without legs. I began to experience something rather like fear.

Suddenly I noticed a twitch of one of the curtains and heard a sound like that of a person jumping about on one leg. I must admit to experiencing alternate sensations of heat and cold, to feeling a strange breeze blowing down my back and to finding my hair pushing up my nightcap.

The curtains parted and there entered the

strangest figure I had ever seen. It was a girl like a dark-skinned Eastern dancing maiden, exquisitely beautiful and typically Egyptian. Her eyes were almond shaped, uptilted at the corners, her eyebrows so black they seemed to be blue; her nose was delicately shaped, almost grecian, and you might have taken her for a bronze statue from Corinth if the prominent cheek bones and the slightly African fullness of the lips had not proclaimed beyond doubt the hieroglyphic race from the banks of the Nile.

Her slim child-like arms were encircled by metal bangles and glass bands. Her hair was finely plaited and at her breast there hung an idol whose seven-thonged whip identified it as Isis, guide of the dead. A golden medal gleamed on her forehead and traces of rouge mingled with the copper tone of her skin.

Her dress was very strange. Imagine a close-fitting sheath of bands embroidered with hieroglyphics of black and red, stiffened with bitumen and belonging, or so it seemed, to a mummy freshly released from its wrappings.

By one of those irrational progressions of ideas so common in dreams, I heard the antiques dealer's hoarse voice saying over and over, like a monotonous refrain, the phrase he had, with so strange an intonation, uttered in his shop: 'Old Pharaoh will not be pleased. He loved his daughter very much, the dear man'.

A curious feature which by no means reassured me was that the apparition had only one foot. The other leg was broken at the ankle.

She moved towards the table where the mummy's foot was jumping about with redoubled energy. When she got there, she leant on the edge and a tear glittered in her eye.

Although she did not speak, I could clearly read her thoughts. She looked at the foot, for it was certainly hers, with an expression of flirtatious sadness and infinite charm, but the foot went on jumping and running hither and thither as if it were impelled by springs of steel.

Twice or thrice she put out her hand to grasp it but it eluded her.

Then, between Princess Hermonthis and the foot, which seemed to be endowed with a life of its own, there began a strange dialogue in an ancient coptic tongue such as might have been spoken, thirty centuries ago, in the tombs of the land of

Ser. Fortunately, that night I could speak coptic to perfection.

In a sweet, vibrant voice like a little crystal bell Princess Hermonthis said: 'Well, my dear little foot, you are still running away although I took good care of you. I bathed you in perfumed water in an alabaster bowl. I polished your heel with a pumice stone dipped in palm oil, your nails were cut with golden scissors and polished with hippopotamus tooth, I chose for you embroidered slippers with turned-back points, the envy of all the girls of Egypt. Your toes wore rings representing the sacred scarab and you carried one of the lightest bodies a lazy foot could hope to carry'. The foot replied, in a sulky voice: 'You know quite well that I am not free. I have been bought and paid for. The old merchant knew what he was doing and he is still annoyed with you for refusing to marry him; now he has his revenge.

'The Arab who broke into your royal tomb in the subterranean level of the metropolis at Thebes was sent by him: he wanted to prevent you from joining the people of darkness in the nether regions. Have you got five gold coins to buy me back?'

'Alas, no. My jewels, my rings, my purses of gold and silver have all been stolen'. replied Princess Hermonthis with a sigh.

At that, I cried out: 'Princess! I have never unfairly held on to anyone's foot.

'You may not possess the five louis I paid for it, but I return it willingly to you. I would be loth to make such a delightful person as the Princess Hermonthis a cripple!'

I uttered this speech in a courtly tone which must have surprised the lovely Egyptian.

She turned towards me, her face full of gratitude. Her eyes lit up with blue glimmers in their depths.

She picked up her foot which now allowed her to do so, like a woman who is about to put on her slipper, and fixed it quickly and skilfully to her leg.

She took three or four steps round the room to make sure she was no longer lame.

'How happy my father will be. He was so distressed about my mutilation, and from the day of my birth he set the whole population to work to make me a tomb so deep that he could keep me intact until the day when all the souls will be weighed in the scales of Amenthi.

'Come with me to my father's. He will welcome you because you have given me back my foot'.

The suggestion seemed quite natural. I put on a dressing gown with a showy design of leaves which gave me a very pharaonic look. I hastily put some Turkish slippers on my feet and told the Princess I was ready to follow her.

Before we left, Princess Hermonthis took from her neck the little green figurine and placed it on the sheets of paper scattered about the table.

'It is only fair I should replace your paper weight' she said.

She held out her hand which was soft and cold like the skin of a viper and off we went.

For a while we sped with the speed of an arrow through a fluid grey substance in which faintly outlined silhouettes passed us on both sides.

For a moment, all we saw was water and sky.

A few moments later, we could see obelisks, monumental doors, stairways surmounted by sphinx-like figures on the horizon.

We had arrived.

The princess led me towards a mountain of pink granite where a low narrow opening would have been impossible to distinguish from cracks in the stone if two steles decorated with sculpture had not been set on either side.

Hermonthis lit a torch and walked on ahead of me.

Corridors were hewn out of the bare rock. The walls, covered in hieroglyphics and allegorical processions must have kept thousands of hands busy for thousands of years. These interminable corridors ended in rooms in the middle of which shafts had been sunk. We descended by means of spiral stairways or spiked footholds. The shafts led us to other rooms from which led other corridors daubed with hawks, snakes coiled into circles, symbols of immortality, a work of such prodigious scope no living human eye should have had the right to behold it. Here were legends without end written in granite that only the dead had time to read in the course of eternity.

We came at last to a room of such vast dimensions it was almost impossible to see the end of it. Monstrous columns stretched in ranks as far as the eye could see, separated by glimmering yellow lights. These revealed prodigious depths below.

Princess Hermonthis still held me by the hand and graciously bowed to the mummies of her acquaintance.

My eyes began to get used to the twilight and I was able to discern the objects by which I was surrounded.

Seated on thrones were the kings of the underworld. There were old men with skin like parchment, blackened with bitumen and naphtha, in golden headdresses, their chests covered in ceremonial necklaces studded with precious stones, their eyes staring like the Sphinx; behind them their servants stood embalmed and rigid in the stiff attitude of Egyptian art, eternally fixed in the pose prescribed by the hieratic code. Behind them cats, ibises and crocodiles mewed, flapped their wings and snapped their jaws, more monstrous than in life, with their bands of mummy cloth.

All the Pharaohs were there - Cheops, Chephrenes, Psammetichus, Sesostris, Amenoteph. All the dark overlords of the pyramids and the rock tombs. On a higher platform sat King Chronos and Xixouthros who was contemporary with the flood, and Tubal Cain, who preceded it. King Xixouthros' beard had grown so much it went seven times round the table he was leaning on, lost in a dream.

In a vaporous cloud sat further on the seventy-two pre-Adamite kings with their seventy-two nations, now gone for ever.

After leaving me to enjoy this intoxicating sight for a few moments, Princess Hermonthis introduced me to her father the Pharaoh who acknowledged my presence with a most majestic nod.

'I've found my foot' cried the princess clapping her hands with delight 'this gentleman gave it back to me'.

The races of Keme and Nahasi, all the black, bronze, copper-coloured nations repeated in chorus: 'Princess Hermonthis has found her foot'. Xixouthros himself was moved to say: 'By Oms, hound of hell, and by Tmei, daughter of the Sun and of Truth, this is a brave and worthy young man'. Holding out towards me his sceptre tipped with a lotus flower, the Pharaoh asked:

'What reward do you seek?'

Emboldened by the audacity of dreams where nothing seems impossible, I asked for the hand of

Hermonthis: a hand for a foot seemed an antithetical reward in rather good taste.

The Pharaoh opened his glass eyes wide, surprised at my jest and my request.

'Where do you come from and how old are you?

'I am French. I am twenty-seven years of age, venerable Pharaoh'

'Twenty-seven, and he wants to marry Princess Hermonthis who is thirty centuries!' cried all the thrones and all the nations.

Only Hermonthis did not seem to find my request unusual.

'If you were only two thousand years old, continued the old king, I would willingly give you the princess' hand in marriage, but the disproportion is too great. Our daughters need husbands who will last. You no longer know how to preserve yourselves. The last to be brought here, scarcely fifteen centuries ago are no more than a handful of ash. Look, my flesh is as hard as basalt, my bones are steel bars.

'I will survive until the end of the world with the body and face I had when I was alive. My daughter Hermonthis will last longer than a bronze statue'.

'When the wind has dispersed the last grain of your dust, Isis herself, who was able to reassemble the remains of Osiris, would be hard put to recompose your being'.

'See how vigorous I am still and how strong my arms are', he said, shaking me by the hand fit to cut off my fingers with my own rings.

He gripped me so tightly I woke up to find my friend Alfred holding my arm and shaking me awake.

'Come on, do I have to carry you out into the street and let off fireworks in your ears to wake you up? It's after twelve; don't you remember you promised to take me to see Monsieur Aguado's Spanish paintings?'

'I'd quite forgotten', I replied, hurrying to dress. 'Let's go. I have the tickets here on my desk'.

Imagine my amazement when instead of the mummy's foot I had bought the day before I saw the little green figurine Princess Hermonthis had put in its place.

THE HAND OF GLORY
by Gérard de Nerval
First published in *Le Cabinet de Lecture*
24 September 1832

THE HAND OF GLORY
1
The place Dauphine

There is no finer sight than that majestic array of seventeenth-century houses in the place Royale. When their stone-edged brick façades and lofty windows are aflame with the glow of the setting sun, you feel the same sense of awe as you might experience in the presence of some parliamentary assembly clad in ermine-trimmed scarlet robes. The comparison may be somewhat naive, but the frame of lime trees which surrounds the square and adds the finishing touch to its sober elegance is like the long green table at which those redoubtable personages are seated.

There is another *place* in the city of Paris whose noble symmetry inspires the beholder with a similar sense of admiration and which represents in the form of a triangle what the first expresses in a square. It was built in the reign of Henri le Grand, who called it the place Dauphine. People were amazed at the speed with which the whole of the Ile de Gourdaine's wasteland was covered with buildings. The invasion was greatly resented by the clerks of the Palais de Justice who gathered there in noisy groups and by the lawyers who came to elaborate their arguments in that spot, so fresh and green after the foul stench of the Law Courts.

Scarcely had those three rows of houses been set up on their substantial porticos, dressed in their brickwork, decorated with stone, pierced by their balustraded windows and crowned with their massive roofs than the whole place was invaded by the legal species, each according to his own means and status, in other words, in inverse relation to the construction of the floors. It became a sort of Cour des Miracles on a grand scale, a bolt-hole for privileged sharks, the haunt of the masters of chicanery just like those other dens frequented by the masters of thieves' cant, the former made of bricks and stone, the latter of wattle and daub.

In one of the houses of the place Dauphine there lived, towards the end of the reign of Henri le Grand a somewhat remarkable character called Godinot Chevassut whose official title was Civil Lieutenant of the Provost of Paris, a responsibility both onerous and lucrative at a time when rogues were more plentiful than they are today, so greatly has probity diminished in our land of France, and when the number of wanton girls was much greater, to such an extent have our morals become depraved. For as one writer puts it, humanity changes so little that the fewer scoundrels there are in the galleys, the more there are elsewhere. It must also be said that the scoundrels of those days were less depraved than those of today and that the trade was at that time a kind of art which young people of good family were not ashamed to embrace. Many a talent suppressed by those outside or on the fringes of a society of privilege could be developed within it; the practitioners were more dangerous to individuals than to the state which might have exploded without this safety-valve. Justice in those days was indulgent towards well-born scoundrels and no one was more tolerant in this respect than our Civil Lieutenant of the place Dauphine, for reasons you will shortly learn. On the other hand, no one was harsher towards the amateur. The latter was a scape-goat for all the others and decorated the gallows-trees with which Paris was at that time shaded, to use an expression of d'Aubigny's, to the great satisfaction of the bourgeoisie who were the more successfully robbed thereby and to the refinement of the art of begging. Godinot Chevassut was a plump little person who was delighted that his hair was beginning to turn grey, unlike most old men, because it lost in so doing the somewhat hectic colour it had always had, earning him the unpleasant nickname *Carrots* commonly used by his acquaintance instead of his real name because it was easier to pronounce and to remember. He also had a tendency to squint although his eyes were constantly on the look-out in spite of being half-closed beneath their bushy brows and his mouth was exceptionally large as is often the case with people who laugh a lot. However, although his features wore an almost permanent expression of amusement, he was never heard to laugh out loud, or, as they say, to laugh like a drain. Every time he uttered something amusing, however, he would punctuate it with a 'ha' or a 'ho' from deep inside his chest, producing a uniquely curious effect. This happened frequently, as he enjoyed peppering his conversation with barbed thrusts, double entendres and ribald comments that he never restrained, even in court. Besides, in those days the legal profession made a habit of that sort of thing: today you only find it in the provinces.

To complete the portrait, imagine a long nose with a square tip set in the usual place, rather small ears without rims and sharp enough to hear the chink of an écu half a mile away and a ten-franc piece much further. It was in this connection that a certain plaintiff, having enquired if Monsieur the Lieutenant Civil did not have friends who might be invited to plead his cause replied that indeed there were friends Carrots thought very highly of. They were Monseigneur Doubloon, Sire Ducat and even Monsieur Ecu. Several had to be involved at the same time and you would then be sure to receive his full attention.

II
An obsession
There are people who esteem highly this or that outstanding characteristic, this or that singular virtue. Some favour magnanimity and bravery on the field of battle and are only happy when they are listening to stories of fine feats of arms. Others rate highest the inventions of science, the arts, letters and such-like manifestations of genius.

Others, yet again, are more affected by generosity and those virtuous actions reflecting devotion to the welfare of our fellow men. Godinot Chevassut's firm conviction was the same as that of wise King Charles IX, namely that no virtue is to be esteemed more highly than wit and presence of mind and that those possessed of these qualities are the only ones deserving of honour and admiration in this world. Nowhere were these characteristics to be found more highly developed than among the great race of coat snatchers, artful dodgers, cut-purses and gypsies whose clever tricks and carefree demeanour came every day to his attention in all their inexhaustible variety.

His hero was Master François Villon, Parisian, as famous in the art of poetry as in the art of picking pockets. He would have given the *Iliad*, the *Aeneid* and the *Romance of Huon of Bordeaux* for the poem *The Freeloaders* and even more for *The Legend of Maitre Faifeu*, which are the epic poetry of the race of vagrants. The *Illustrations of Du Bellay*, Aristotle's *Peripoliticon* and the *Cymbalum Mundi* seemed to him very feeble compared with *Jargon*, followed by *The States General of the Kingdom of Argot* and *The*

Dialogues of the Knave and the Malingerer by a bottle walloper working in the town of Tours and printed by permission of the King of Thunes (Fiacre the Packman, Tours 1603). And of course, as those who vaunt a particular virtue have the greatest contempt for the opposite vice, none were so contemptible in his eyes as ordinary people of limited understanding. He had reached the stage where he would have liked to change the whole course of justice so that when he came across some serious piece of roguery he would have hanged the victim, not the robber. According to him, this would hasten the intellectual emancipation of the people and enable them to reach that degree of mental agility, quickness of apprehension and inventiveness which he considered to be the true crown of humanity and a state of perfection most pleasing to God. So much for the theory. As for the practice. he was convinced that theft organised on a grand scale was the best way of dividing up great fortunes and passing round smaller ones, as a result of which the lower classes would enjoy freedom and well-being.

Of course, only really gilt-edged trickery

delighted him, the subtleties and verbal brilliance of the real band of Saint Nicholas, the old tricks of Maître Gonin the conjuror, preserved for two hundred years in the salt of wit; Villon the villain was his mentor, not Captain Crossroads or the Guilleris brothers. For sure, the scoundrel who brutally robs an unarmed traveller on the highway was as abhorrent to him as to all well-meaning people as much as those who without any effort of the imagination break into some isolated house, steal the contents and often kill the inhabitants. But if he had heard about a distinguished rascal who made a hole in a wall to enable him to enter a house and shaped it like a gothic trefoil so that the next day when the theft was discovered it could be seen to have been committed by a man of taste, Maître Godinot Chevassut would have held him in higher esteem than Bertrand de Clasquin or Julius Caesar, that's for certain.

III
The Magistrate's Bags
Having said that, I think it is time to raise the curtain and following the old custom to administer a kick in the pants to Master Prologue who has

become insufferably prolix, so much so that the candles have been snuffed out three times since he began his speech. Let him then make an end, like Bruscambille urging the spectators to 'clean up the imperfections of his speech with the dusters of their humanity and to administer an enema of excuses to the intestines of their impatience'. Now that we have done so, the action can begin.

The room is large, dark and wood-panelled. The old magistrate is seated in a great carved armchair with ornamental legs whose back is covered in fringed damask. He is trying on a pair of baggy breeches just delivered by Eustache Bouteroue, the apprentice of Maître Goubard, draper and breeches-maker. Fastening his laces, Maître Chevassut gets up and sits down several times in succession speaking from time to time to the young man who has been invited to perch on the edge of a stool and sits there watching him timidly like a plaster saint.

'They have served their time', says the magistrate, kicking away the old breeches he has just taken off. 'They were at the end of their thread, like a court judgment. All the parts were saying goodbye to one another, a heart-rending goodbye'.

The facetious old man picked up the worn-out garment and took out his purse from which he selected a few coins.

'It is certain,' said he, 'that we men of the legal profession make our clothes last because of the robe we wear over them. This is why, since everyone must live, even thieves and drapers, I will not deduct anything from the six écus Maître Goubard is charging. I will even add one écu for the messenger boy, a clipped one, on condition he will not let it go cheap but pass it off for one of full value to some good-for-nothing bourgeois, using to that effect all the cunning he possesses. Otherwise I will keep it for next Sunday's collection at Notre Dame.'

Eustache Bouteroue took the six écus and the clipped one and made a deep bow.

'Well now, my lad, are we beginning to get the hang of the drapery business? Are we learning how to sell a short length and pass off old cloth for new, dark brown for black? Are we keeping up the reputation of the Halles traders?'

Eustache looked up in alarm at the magistrate, then thinking he was joking began to laugh. But the magistrate was not laughing.

'I am not keen on shopkeepers who rob their customers', he added. 'The thief steals and does so without pretence. The shopkeeper steals and conceals his dishonesty. A man with the gift of the gab and a knowledge of Latin buys a pair of breeches. He haggles over the price and ends up paying six écus. Then an honest Christian soul comes along, the sort some people call a simpleton, others a decent fellow. If he happens to buy a pair of breeches exactly the same as the first man's and trusting the draper who swears by the Virgin and all the saints that he is an honest man, pays him eight écus, I have no sympathy for him because he's a fool. But when the shopkeeper, counting up the money he has received from the two customers, jingles the two écus difference in his pocket with satisfaction, sees a poor man on his way to the galleys for stealing a filthy old handkerchief from someone's pocket and says, holding his two écus in his hand: *There goes a scoundrel and a half! If justice were truly just that man would be broken on the wheel and I would go and watch*, what do you think would happen, Eustache, if justice were truly just?'

Eustache Bouteroue stopped laughing. The

paradox was too strange for him to venture a reply and the mouth it came out of rather disturbing. Maître Chevassut, seeing the young man was bamboozled, like a wolf in a trap, began to laugh his special laugh, gave him a little tap on the cheek and sent him on his way. Eustache came down the stone stairs in a thoughtful frame of mind although he could hear from the yard of the Palais de Justice the sound of the trumpet of Galinette the Galine, clown of the famous Geronimo who attracted great crowds by his antics and persuaded them to buy his master's quack remedies. He made a point of going back to the Halles by way of the Pont Neuf.

IV
The Pont Neuf
The Pont Neuf, finished in the reign of Henry IV, is the chief monument to that monarch. Nothing can describe the enthusiasm it aroused when, after years of toil it crossed the Seine in twelve strides and linked more closely the three cities of the capital. It soon became the rendez-vous of all the idlers of Paris, of whom great is the number, and consequently, of all the strolling players, sellers of potions and pickpockets whose trade was much

increased by the new highway just as a mill wheel is set in motion by a rushing stream.

When Eustache left the triangle of the place Dauphine the sun was beating down on the bridge thronged with people, for the most populous of all the streets of Paris are those whose only blossoms are the stalls of traders, whose terraces are made of paving stones and whose shade is afforded only by high walls and and houses.

Eustache navigated with difficulty the great stream of people crossing that other stream of the Seine and flowing slowly from one end of the bridge to the other, held up by the slightest obstacle, like ice-floes carried along by the current, separating here and there into a thousand tributaries and a thousand whirlpools around certain conjurors, singers or merchants trading their wares. Many stopped at the parapet to watch the logs floating by beneath the arches and the boats sailing past or to gaze at the wonderful view of the Seine downstream from the bridge, the Seine flowing past the long line of buildings of the Louvre on the right and on the left the great Pré aux-Clercs, criss-crossed by its fine avenues of lime trees, framed by its shaggy grey willows weeping into the water, then on either side, the Tour de Nesle and the Tour du Bois which seemed to stand guard over the gates of Paris like giants in a fairy tale.

Suddenly a great burst of fireworks attracted the attention of all the strollers and sightseers with its promise of a noteworthy spectacle.

It was in the middle of one of those little half-moon-shaped platforms lately surmounted by shops which are now empty spaces above each pier of the bridge, to the side of the roadway. Here, a conjuror had set up his table and a very handsome monkey was walking round it dressed in a black and red devil suit with his tail protruding. He was setting off fire-crackers and Catherine wheels to the detriment of all the beards and starched collars standing too close.

Its master had one of those gipsy faces which had been common a hundred years before, were already rare at the time of this story and today have almost vanished, submerged in the ugliness and insignificance of our bourgeois features: a hatchet face with a high straight brow, a long hooked nose not curving down like a Roman nose but turned up instead, scarcely overhanging the mouth with its thin, pushed-out lips and a receding chin. The eyes were long and upward-slanting beneath V-shaped eyebrows and the whole was framed in long black hair. Something supple and relaxed in the gestures and the whole body suggested a wily and resourceful individual, loose limbed and schooled from childhood in many different trades and skills.

He wore with dignity an old clown suit with a wide-brimmed hat much creased and crumpled. Everyone called him Maître Gonin either because of his skills or because he really did descend from that famous entertainer who founded the theatre of the Children of Fun and was the first to bear the title King of Fools which at the time of this tale had passed to the Seigneur Engoulevent who carried its prerogatives as far as the Houses of Parliament.

V
Fortune Telling

When the juggler saw a goodly number of people gathered together he began to perform a few tricks with the drinking glasses which excited noisy admiration. It is true that the entertainer had chosen his pitch in the half-moon recess deliberately, and not merely to avoid disturbing the traffic, as it seemed. By so doing, he ensured he had spectators only in front of him, not behind. For in fact the art had not yet progressed to the stage it has reached today, when the juggler works surrounded by his public. When the trick with the goblets was done, the monkey went the rounds, picking up a good deal of small change and thanking the audience with a gallant bow accompanied by a little high-pitched squeak like the noise made by a cricket. But the goblets, or drinking glasses, were only the prelude to something else and in a well-turned prologue, Maître Gonin announced that he had the gift of foretelling the future by means of the cards, reading palms and pythagorean numbers. These things were above price, he said, but he would do it for a sou, merely to oblige people. As he spoke, he shuffled a large pack of cards and the monkey, who was called Pacolet, gave them out in a very clever way to all those holding out their hands.

When he had satisfied all requests for cards, his master called the clients into the half-moon by the name of the cards they held and foretold to each his good or bad fortune. Meanwhile, Pacolet, to whom he had given an onion in recompense for his services, amused the company by the contortions this feast occasioned him, being at once delighted and uncomfortable, laughing with his mouth and weeping with his eyes, growling with pleasure as he chewed the onion and grimacing pitiably at the effect it had.

Eustache Bouteroue, who had also taken a card, was the last to be called. Maître Gonin looked carefully at his long naive face and addressed him authoritatively:

'This is your past: you have lost your parents. You have been apprenticed for the last six years to a draper doing business in the colonnade of the Halles. This is your present: your master has promised you his only daughter in marriage. He plans to retire and leave you his business. Now for the future. Show me your hand.'

Surprised, Eustache held out his hand. The juggler examined the lines with interest, frowned with an air of hesitation and called his monkey over as if to consult him. The monkey took the hand, looked at it, then, jumping over his master's shoulder, seemed to whisper in his ear. But all he was doing was moving his lips very quickly as animals do when they are not pleased.

'That's funny!' said Maître Gonin at last. 'Strange that such a simple life, beginning in so ordinary a way, should end so uncommonly, moving towards such a lofty aim. Ah, my young cockerel, you will break your shell; you will go high, very high... you will die greater than you are.'

'That's what these people always promise you', said Eustache to himself. 'But how does he know the things he told me in the first place? That's remarkable, unless he's seen me somewhere before.

However, he took from his pocket the magistrate's clipped écu, asking the juggler to give him his change. Perhaps he spoke too quietly, as the latter did not hear him and he continued, rolling the écu about between his fingers:

'I can see you are a man of taste so I will add a few details to the prediction I made, which was very accurate but somewhat ambiguous. Yes, my friend, you did not offer a sou like the others, although your écu lacks a quarter; never mind, this silver coin will be a bright mirror in which the simple truth will be revealed to you.'

'So what you told me about my elevation was not the truth?'

'You asked me to tell your fortune and I have done so, but the glossary was missing... How do you interpret the lofty aim I gave your existence in my prediction?'

'I deduce that I will become a member of the guild of master drapers, a parish councillor, a magistrate...'

'That would be the day!... Why not the Grand Cham of Tartary into the bargain? Oh no, my friend; you are on the wrong track, and as you require an explanation of this sybilline oracle I can tell you that in our parlance, *to go high* refers to those sent to tend sheep on the moon, just as *to go far* is for those sent to write their story in the waters, with fifteen foot pens...'

'All right, but if you could explain your explanation a bit, I would certainly understand.'

'They are truthful expressions to replace the words *gibbet* and *galleys*. You will go high and I will go far. In my case, it is perfectly shown by this median line crossed at right angles by other fainter lines. In your case, by a line that meets the middle one without going beyond it and another obliquely crossing them both.'

'The gibbet'! cried Eustache.

'Are you really set on a horizontal death?' asked Maître Gonin. 'That would be childish, all the more so because you can be sure of escaping all sorts of other deaths to which every mortal man is exposed. Besides, it is possible that when Milord Gibbet lifts you up by the neck with his outstreched arm you will be an old man, sick and tired of the world. But it is noon and therefore time when the order of the Provost of Paris excludes us from the Pont Neuf until nightfall. Now if you ever need advice, a spell, a charm or a philtre in case of danger or a love affair or a matter of revenge, I live over there at the end of the bridge in the Chateau-Gaillard. Can you see that little tower...'? 'Just one more thing, please', said Eustache, trembling, 'Will I have a happy marriage?'

'Bring me your wife and I will tell you...Pacolet, a bow for the gentleman and kiss his hand.'

The juggler folded up his table, tucked it under his arm, put the monkey on his shoulder and set off for the Chateau-Gaillard humming a very old tune between his teeth.

VI
Trials and Tribulations

It is quite true that Eustache Bouteroue was soon to be married to the draper's daughter. He was a sensible lad, well up in matters of business, using his free time not in playing bowls or tennis, like many others, but doing accounts, reading The Book of the Six Corporations of Paris, and learning a little Spanish which in those days a tradesman did well to study, just as nowadays it is a good idea to speak English, because of the great number of people of that country who live in Paris. Having convinced himself over the past six years of the perfect honesty and excellent character of his apprentice, having detected between his daughter and the apprentice a certain virtuous and severely controlled attraction, Maître Goubard had decided to arrange their marriage on Midsummer Day and then to retire to Laon in Picardy where he had family possessions.

Eustache had no money of his own but in those days it was not the custom to marry one money bag with another. Sometimes the parents consulted the inclinations of the young people and took the trouble to study the character, behaviour and capabilities of those with whom they intended to join them in matrimony. Very different from the parents of today who require greater moral guarantees from a servant than from a son-in-law.

The prediction of the juggler had so concentrated the ideas of the apprentice draper that he remained for some time in a state of bewilderment in the recess on the bridge and did not hear the silvery voices prattling in the belfries of the Samaritaine repeating twelve o'clock. But in Paris twelve o'clock goes on ringing for an hour. The clock of the Louvre soon spoke up more solemnly, then the one at the Grands Augustins, then the Châtelet, so that Eustache, terrified at being so late, began to run as fast as he could and in a few minutes had left behind him the rue de la Monnaie, the rue Borrel and the rue Tirechappe. Then he slowed down and when he had come round the rue de la Boucherie de Beauvais he stopped frowning when he saw the red umbrellas of the Halles, the stage of the Enfants sans Souci, the ladder, the cross and the pretty lantern of the pillory surmounted by its lead roof. It was on this square, beneath one of those umbrellas, that his fiancée, Javotte Goubard was waiting for him to return. Most of the shopkeepers on the colonnade had a stall on the pavement of the Halles, kept by a representative of the shop and forming a branch of their dark premises. Javotte took her place there every morning and sometimes as she sat amid the merchandise she would work at making shoulder knots or stand up to address the passers by, seize their arm and not let go until they had made some purchase. This did not prevent her from being the shyest young girl imaginable; graceful, pretty, blonde, tall and leaning slightly forward like most young girls in business whose figure is slim and fragile, blushing like a strawberry at the slightest thing outside the daily business of the stall but on that score the equal of any trader on the pavement in her market patter.

At twelve, Eustache would usually replace her beneath the red umbrella while she went in to have dinner with her father. He was afraid Javotte might be growing impatient but as soon as he caught sight of her she looked as calm as calm could be, leaning on a roll of cloth and listening very attentively to the conversation of a handsome soldier who was leaning against the same roll and looked no more like a shopkeeper than you can possibly imagine.

'This is my fiancé, said Javotte, smiling up at the stranger who nodded his head slightly without moving from where he was standing close to Javotte. He merely looked the apprentice up and down with the disdain soldiers affect in the presence of bourgeois individuals of insignificant appearance.

'He looks a bit like one of our buglers', he said without a smile,'only he has thinner legs; but you know, Javotte, in a squadron the bugler is a bit less than a horse and a bit more than a dog...'

'This is my nephew', said Javotte to Eustache turning her big blue eyes towards him with a smile. 'He has been granted leave to attend our wedding, isn't that nice? He's an arquebusier.... What a fine body of men! If you were dressed like that, Eustache.... but you aren't tall enough or strong enough...'

'And how long will monsieur do us the honour of staying in Paris?' asked the young man timidly.

'That depends', said the soldier, drawing himself up to his full height, after keeping Eustache waiting for his answer. 'We were sent to Berri to exterminate the peasants' revolt and if they keep quiet a bit longer, it could be a good month but in any case, at Martinmas we will be coming to Paris to replace the regiment of M. de Humières so I will be able to come and see you every day for an indefinite period'.

Eustache examined the arquebusier as closely as he could without meeting his eyes and judged his physical appearance to be out of all proportion to what is expected of a nephew.

'When I say every day', continued the soldier, 'I am mistaken, for on Thursday the grand parade takes place... but we have the evening to ourselves and I can always come and have supper with you on Thursday'.

'Is he expecting to have dinner on the other days?' thought Eustache... 'But you never told me, Mademoiselle Goubard, that your nephew was such...'

'Such a handsome man? Oh yes, how he has grown! It must be seven years since we saw him last, poor Joseph, and a lot of water has flowed under the bridge since then'.

'And a lot of wine under his nose', thought the apprentice, dazzled by the resplendent countenance of his future nephew. 'You don't get such a rosy complexion with coloured water and

Maître Goubard's bottles will dance the dance of death before the wedding and maybe afterwards as well...'

'Let's go and have dinner, papa must be getting impatient!' said Javotte. 'Take my arm, Joseph. To think that I was once the tallest when I was twelve and you ten; I was the little mother! How proud I shall feel on the arm of an arquebusier! You will take me out, won't you? I go out so little; I'm not allowed out alone and on Sunday evening I have to go to evening service because I am a Child of Mary, at the Holy Innocents Church; I have to carry one of the ribbons...'

Soon, this girlish chatter, punctuated by the ringing step of the soldier, the graceful, slight form dancing along on the arm of the man's burly upright one, disappeared into the muffling darkness of the colonnade bordering the rue de la Tonnellerie and Eustache was left with a mist in his eyes and a humming in his ears.

VII
Tribulations and Trials

So far we have kept up step by step with the action of this bourgeois epic without spending longer in the telling than it took in the performance. Now, in spite of our respect, or rather our profound esteem, for the observation of the unities, even in story-telling, we must make a leap of a few days. Eustache's tribulations with regard to his nephew by marriage would be quite interesting to relate but were less of a problem than one might imagine. Eustache was soon reassured as far as his fiancée was concerned: all Javotte had done was to retain a rather rosy impression of her childhood experiences, which, in a life as tranquil as hers, had assumed an unusual importance. All she had seen at first in the arquebusier was the noisy, happy child who was once her playmate. She soon noticed that the child had grown up, that he had changed. She became more reserved with him.

As for the soldier, apart from one or two familiarities that were only to be expected, he showed no unworthy intentions towards his young aunt. He was even one of that fairly common type of person in whom honest women inspire very little interest. In any case, like Tabarin, he said that the bottle was his mistress. For the first three days of his stay, he never left Javotte's side and even took her in the evenings to the Cours la Reine accompanied only by the serving wench of the household, to Eustache's considerable dissatisfaction. But it didn't last; he soon grew tired of her company and began to go out alone during the day, not forgetting, of course, to return home at meal times.

The only thing that worried the husband-to-be was to see this relative so well established in the house that was to be his after the wedding that it would not be easy to prise him out gently, for every day he seemed to become more and more of a fixture. However, he was only Javotte's nephew by marriage, being the child of a daughter Maître Goubard had had by a previous marriage. How could he make him understand that he was exaggerating the ties of family relationship and that he had a view of the rights and privileges of family responsibility that were too generous, too precise and too patriarchal?

However it was probable that he would soon become aware of his indiscretion of his own accord and Eustache found himself obliged to be patient, *like the ladies of Fontainebleau when the court is in Paris*, as the old proverb says.

But long after the wedding the arquebusier was still in residence. He even expressed the hope that, thanks to the inactivity of the revolting peasants, he would be able to stay in Paris until the rest of his corps arrived. Eustache tried out a few witticisms to the effect that some people took shops for hotels and certain others which were not apparently understood. Besides, he did not dare to speak openly about it to his wife and father-in-law not wishing to give the impression, in the early days of his marriage, that he was merely a fortune-hunter, he who owed everything to them.

Moreover, the soldier's company was not in the least amusing, his mouth uttered nothing but a long paean to his own glory, founded partly on his exploits in battle which made him the terror of the enemy and partly on his prowess against the peasants, unfortunate people against whom the soldiers of Henry waged war because they failed to pay their taxes and who seemed unlikely ever to enjoy the famous Sunday chicken promised to all his peasantry by the noble monarch.

This boastful style was at the time fairly common, as we can judge from the characters of popular fiction of the day, such as Taillebras and

Captain Matamores. I believe they owe something to the victorious invasion of Paris by the Gascons, following that of the men from Navarre. The type became gradually less obtrusive and a few years later the Baron de Funeste was a watered-down version, more amusing into the bargain, and finally, Corneille's comedy *Le Menteur* has reduced it to acceptable proportions.

What shocked Eustache most in the soldier's behaviour was a tendency to treat him as a little boy, to make pointed remarks about his appearance and to put him in an unfavourable and ridiculous light in the eyes of his wife, which was most disadvantageous at a time when a new husband needs to establish his position and look to the future.

One other subject of irritation became the last straw. As Eustache had been asked to join the traders' neighbourhood watch association and did not want to carry out his duties, like old Maître Goubard, in ordinary clothes, with a halberd lent by the local police, he had bought a sword that had lost its hilt, a helmet and a coat of mail that already needed the services of a blacksmith and having spent three days cleaning and polishing them, he managed to make the metal a little more lustrous than it had been before. But when he put it on and walked about in it proudly in the shop, asking if he didn't look impressive in this get-up, the arquebusier began to laugh like a heap of flies in the sun and told him he looked as if he were wearing the kitchen pots and pans.

VIII
A Flick of the Finger

It so happened that one day, the 12th or the 13th of the month, a Thursday in any case, Eustache closed the shop early, a thing he would not have presumed to do if Maître Goubard had not been absent, having left the previous day to view his property in Picardy as he planned to take up residence there three months later when his successor had solidly established himself in his stead and was thoroughly conversant with the business.

Returning that evening as usual, the arquebusier found the door shut and the lights out. He was much surprised, because the night watch had not yet sounded at the Châtelet and as he never returned home sober, his irritation expressed itself in the form of a mighty oath that shook Eustache in his entresol apartment which, to his own amazement, he had decided to use for the first time as the conjugal bedroom.

'Hey you!' shouted the soldier, kicking the door, 'are we celebrating tonight? Is it St Michael's day, the feast of drapers, coat-snatchers and pickpockets?'

He beat on the shop front with his fist but it had no more effect than if he had poured water into a sieve.

'Hey, uncle and aunt... do you want me to lie down on the pavement for all the dogs of the district to piss on? Devil take relations.....

'What pigs.... get down here fast, bourgeois, here's money for you!... you dirty little so and so... Let me in...'

The door was not in the slightest moved by this discourse. He was wasting his words, like the Venerable Bede preaching to a heap of stones.

But if doors are deaf, windows are not blind and there is a very simple way of helping them to see better. The soldier worked this out for himself, stood back from the dark shadows of the colonnade and from the middle of the rue de la

Tonnellerie, picking up a pebble, aimed it so well that it broke one of the little windows of the entresol. Eustache had never considered the possibility of this powerful question mark being added to the soldier's monologue of *why are you not opening the door?*

Eustache suddenly made up his mind. A coward who gets worked up about something is like a poor man who suddenly starts spending - he takes things to the extreme.

Moreover, Eustache wanted to show his new wife what he was capable of, for once, after she had seen him treated so disrespectfully for some time and used by the soldier as a quintain, with the difference that the quintain sometimes returns hefty blows to those who continually use it. He put on his hat and ran down the narrow stairs of his entresol before Javotte had time to stop him. He picked up his rapier on his way through the back shop and only when he felt the cold brass handle in his hand did he stop for a moment then made his way with leaden feet towards his door, the key to which he held in his other hand. But the sound of a second window breaking and his wife's footsteps behind his own gave him back all his energy; he wrenched open the massive door and planted himself on the doorstep with his naked sword in his hand like the archangel on the threshold of the earthly paradise.

'What's with this night bird, this low life good-for-nothing?' he shouted in a voice which, two notes lower would have quivered uncertainly. 'So this is how you treat honest folk? Turn yourself around and go sleep in the charnel house along the road or I'll call the neighbours and the night watch".

'So that's your tack, numskull? Have you changed your tune? At least it's different.. I love hearing you ranting like that.... heroes are my speciality... Come let me embrace you, brave warrior..'

'Be off with you, villain, the neighbours can hear you and will have you arrested for disturbing the peace. Clear off and don't come back'.

On the contrary, the soldier advanced towards him from between the columns, which slightly spoiled the last words of Eustache's reply.

'Good advice!' said the soldier. 'It deserves paying for'.

Before you could count up to two, he had

flicked his finger and thumb against the young draper's nose fit to turn it scarlet.

'Keep the lot, if you have no change, and thank you for nothing, uncle'.

Eustache could not endure this affront, which was more humiliating than a slap in the face, with his new wife looking on, so notwithstanding her attempts to restrain him, he flung himself upon his adversary and thrust his sword at him in a way that would have done credit to a valiant knight if the sword had been a good one, but it had not had any practice since the Wars of Religion and made no impression on the soldier's buffalo-skin waistcoat. The soldier grabbed his two hands in his in such a way that the sword fell to the ground and then the victim began to shout at the top of his voice, the while kicking furiously at the soft leather boots of his adversary.

Fortunately Javotte got between them for the neighbours were enjoying the spectacle from their windows but had no intention of coming down to stop it. Pulling his blue fingers out of the human vice which had been gripping them, he had to rub them a long time before they resumed their natural shape and colour.

'I am not afraid of you', he shouted, 'and we will meet again. Be at the Pré aux Clercs tomorrow if you have any spunk in you... Till six o'clock, you scoundrel and it's to the death, you louse!'

'An excellent choice of venue, my little prize-fighter. We'll cross swords like gentlemen. Till tomorrow! and by Saint George, it will be too soon for you'. The soldier uttered these words in a tone of consideration he had not shown till then. Eustache turned round proudly towards his wife. His invitation to the duel had increased his height by several inches. He picked up his sword and loudly slammed the door.

IX
The Chateau Gaillard

When he woke up, the young draper found all his courage had evaporated. He had no hesitation in admitting that he had made himself look very stupid by challenging an arquebusier to a duel when the only weapon he could use was a measuring stick with which he had often fenced at the time of his apprenticeship with his friends in the clos des Chartreux. He therefore wasted no time in deciding to stay at home and leave his adversary to play the greenhorn on the Pré aux Clercs swaying back and forth on his heels like a ninny.

When the time had gone by, he got up, opened the shop and said nothing to his wife about last night's scene, just as she, for her part, made no reference to it. They had breakfast in silence, after which Javotte went as usual to sit beneath the red umbrella leaving her husband busy with his servant, examining a piece of cloth for imperfections. It must be said that he often looked towards the door in case his redoubtable relation came to reproach him with his cowardice and failure to keep his word. About half past eight he glimpsed at a distance the uniform of the arquebusier approaching along the colonnade in deep shadow, like one of Rembrandt's warriors, lit only by three points of light, on the helmet, the coat of mail and the nose. It was a sinister apparition which grew taller and clearer by the second and whose metallic tread seemed to beat out each minute of the draper's last hour.

But the same uniform did not cover the same form and to put the matter more simply, the man who stopped in front of Eustache's shop was a soldier colleague of the other. He addressed him in a tone of calm politeness.

He informed him that his adversary, having waited for two hours at the place of rendezvous without his appearing and concluding that an unexpected occurrence had prevented him from turning up, would return the next day at the same time and if the same thing happened he would then come to the shop, cut off both his ears and put them in his pocket as the famous Brusquet had done in 1605 to an equerry of the duc de Chevreuse for the same reason, an action applauded by the court and generally judged to be in excellent taste.

Eustache replied that his adversary underestimated his courage by threatening him in this way and that he now had two scores to settle. He added that the only obstacle was that he had not yet found anyone willing to act as his second.

The other seemed satisfied with this explanation and was kind enough to inform him that he would find excellent seconds on the Pont Neuf in front of the Samaritaine where they usually took their walk. They were people who had no other profession and who were prepared, for an écu, to take on the cause of whoever approached them and even to bring swords. After making these observations, he bowed deeply and withdrew.

Left alone, Eustache began to think the matter over and remained for a long time in a state of perplexity. He hesitated between three courses of action. First to inform the Lieutenant Civil about the soldier's demands and threats and ask his permission to bear arms to defend himself. However, that would still end in a confrontation. Then he made up his mind to put in an appearance at the rendezvous but warn the police in advance so that they would arrive just as the duel was about to begin. The trouble was they could arrive when it had finished! Thirdly, he considered going to see the gipsy of the Pont Neuf, and that is what he finally decided to do.

At twelve the servant took over from Javotte beneath the umbrella and the latter came in to have dinner with her husband. He did not tell her about the visit he had just received but asked her to look after the shop while he went to see a gentleman recently arrived in Paris who wanted a new wardrobe. He took his bag of samples and went off to the Pont Neuf.

The Chateau Gaillard, by the water's edge at the southern extremity of the bridge was a little building surmounted by a round tower which had been a prison in its time but was now beginning to fall into ruin and was only inhabited by poor folk who had no other home. After walking uncertainly for some time among the stones with which the ground was covered, Eustache found a little door to the centre of which a bat had been nailed. He knocked gently and Maître Gonin's monkey immediately opened the door, a job for which he had been trained, as are some domestic cats.

The conjuror was sitting reading at a table. He turned round and gestured to the young man to sit down on a stool. When the latter had told him what had happened, he told him it was the simplest thing in the world, but that he had done well to consult him.

'You need a charm', he said, 'a magic charm to help you defeat your adversary, don't you'?

'Certainly, if it is possible'!

'Although everybody tries to do it, you will never find spells as good as mine. They are not formed by black magic, like the others, but result from a profound study of white magic and do not in any way compromise the health of the soul'.

'That's all right then', said Eustache, 'otherwise I would never have anything to do with them. But how much does your magic cost? I must know if I will be able to afford it'. 'Understand that what you are buying is life, and glory into the bargain. Do you imagine that for those two wonderful things I could ask less than a hundred écus?'

'A hundred devils take you!' growled Eustache, his face darkening. 'That's more than I possess. What use will life be to me without bread, and glory without clothes?' In any case it may be a false promise for gullible people'.

'You will not have to pay till later'.

'That's something.. what sort of security do you want'?

'Just your hand'.

'Really? I must be a fool to listen to your nonsense. Did you not tell me I would end up on the gallows?'

'Certainly. And I do not go back on it.'

'Well then, if that's the case, what have I to fear from the duel?'

'Nothing, except a few gashes and the odd stab

to open wider the doors of your soul.. After that you will be picked up and hoisted high all the same, dead or alive and so your destiny will be complete. Do you understand?'

The draper understood so well that he hastened to offer his hand to the juggler as a token of consent asking him to grant him ten days to find the money, to which the other agreed after making a note on the wall of the date fixed for payment. Then he took the book of Albertus Magnus with commentaries by Agrippa and the abbé Trithème, opened it at the article on single combat and to assure Eustache that there would be nothing diabolical about what he was going to do, told him that he could say his prayers without it affecting the spell. Then he lifted up the lid of a box, took out an unglazed pot and mixed together in it divers ingredients indicated in the book, repeating in a low voice a kind of incantation. When he had finished he took Eustache's right hand which was making the sign of the cross, and anointed it up to the wrist with the mixture he had just prepared.

Then he took out of the box a very old greasy flask and slowly tilting it spread a few drops on the back of the hand, uttering Latin words which resembled those used by priests for baptism.

Only then did Eustache feel a sort of tingling like an electric shock along the whole of his arm, which alarmed him. His hand felt numb and yet, strangely enough, it began to twist and stretch out to crack its joints several times like an animal waking up, then he felt nothing more, the circulation seemed to return to normal and Maître Gonin said it was all over and that now he could defy the finest swordsmen of the court and the army and make them buttonholes for all the useless buttons with which fashion overloaded their clothes.

X
The Pré Aux Clercs

The next morning, four men were walking about in the green alleys of the Pré aux Clercs looking for a suitably secluded spot. When they reached the foot of the little slope bordering the southern part, they stopped on a bowls pitch which seemed a very good place to engage in a duel. Then Eustache and his adversary took off their jackets and the seconds examined them according to custom, under the shirt and under the breeches. The draper was not exactly unafraid, but he trusted the gipsy's charm for it is well known that magic spells, charms, philtres and bewitchments have never been so widely trusted as at that time, when they gave rise to so many trials, of which the parliamentary records are full, and in which judges shared the general belief.

Eustache's witness, whom he had engaged on the Pont Neuf and paid one écu, greeted the arquebusier's friend and asked him if he intended to fight too. When the latter replied that he did not, he folded his arms and drew back preparing to admire the champions at work.

The draper could not help feeling rather sick when his adversary made the salute with the foils, which he did not return. He stood stock still, holding his sword in front of him like a candle, and his posture was so bad that the soldier, who was not ungenerous, resolved to do no more than scratch him. But scarcely had they touched rapiers than Eustache noticed that his hand was pulling his arm forward and flinging itself about mightily. To be exact, he was only aware of it by the powerful pressure it exerted on the muscles of his arm. Its movements had a prodigious power and energy which could be compared to that of a steel spring. The soldier's wrist was almost dislocated when he parried the tierce, but the quarte sent his sword flying while Eustache's sword, without a pause and in the same movement ran through his body so violently that the hilt came right down on his chest. Eustache, who had not lunged and who had been carried along by an unexpected jolt, would have split his head open when he fell full length if he had not landed on the adversary's belly.

'God's body! What a wrist'! cried the soldier's second. 'That lad could teach the chevalier Tord-Chêne a thing or two! He lacks grace and physique but that arm is more deadly than a Welsh longbow.'

Eustache, however, had got up with the help of his second and for a moment remained absorbed in what had just happened. But when he became fully aware of the arquebusier stretched out at his feet, nailed to the ground by the sword, like a toad inside a magic circle, he took to his heels so fast that he left his Sunday coat with its silk braid lying on the ground.

Now as the soldier was well and truly dead, the

two seconds had nothing to gain by remaining at the scene and made off. They had gone a hundred yards or so when Eustache's man suddenly exclaimed: 'I've forgotten the sword I lent!'

He left the other man to go on his way and when he returned to the scene of combat, began to turn out the pockets of the dead man, finding only some keys, a bit of string and a much-used pack of tarot cards.

'Not a thing!' he murmured, 'just another knave without money or a watch. Devil take you, arquebusier!'

Not daring to take away the uniform, as he would be compromised by selling it, our man merely removed the soldier's boots, rolled them up under his cape with Eustache's jacket and went on his way cursing and complaining.

XI
Obsession

For many days the draper never went out, devastated by that tragic death which he had brought about for the most insignificant of offences and in a way that was as damnable in this world as the next. At times, he wondered if it were all a dream and were it not for his missing Sunday jacket, an irrefutable witness that stood out by its very absence, he might have questioned the reliability of his memory.

One evening he felt he wanted to confront the evidence and went along to the Pré aux Clercs, ostensibly for a walk. His eyes faltered when he saw the bowls pitch where the duel had taken place and he was obliged to sit down. Some lawyers were enjoying a game as they often did before supper, and as soon as the mist had cleared from his eyes, Eustache thought he could see a great pool of blood on the ground between the feet of one of the players.

He rose unsteadily to his feet and hurried out of the park, the blood stain constantly before his eyes without changing shape, superimposing itself everywhere he looked as he walked along, like those spots of light you see hovering about after you have glanced up at the sun.

When he got home, he thought he had been followed and it was only then he recalled that some people at Queen Marguerite's House, which he had passed the other morning and again that very evening, might have recognised him.

Although the duelling laws were at that time not executed rigorously, it occurred to him that it might be generally considered a good idea to hang a poor shopkeeper as a warning to Court Society for no one dared attack them at that time as they did later.

These thoughts along with several others gave him a very sleepless night. He could not close his eyes an instant without seeing a thousand gibbets shaking their fists at him, with a dead man hanging at the end of a rope and laughing hideously or a skeleton showing all its ribs against a great yellow moon.

Then a good idea occurred to him, sweeping away all those distorted visions. Eustache suddenly remembered the Lieutenant Civil, an old customer of his father-in-law who had already been quite affable with him. He resolved to go and see him the next day and to tell all, convinced that he would protect him if only for the sake of Javotte whom as a baby, he had dandled on his knee and Maître Gobard of whom he thought highly. The poor merchant at last fell asleep and rested, till morning, on the pillow of this good resolution. At about nine the next day he knocked on the magistrate's door. The valet de chambre admitted him at once, supposing he had come to measure up his master for some new clothes or to offer something for sale.

Reclining comfortably in a great wing armchair, the magistrate was reading with relish the old poem of Merlin Coccaie, particularly enjoying the adventures of Balde, worthy prototype of Pantagruel, and even more so the unrivalled tricks and stratagems of Cingar, that grotesque character on whom our own Panurge was so successfully modelled.

Maître Chevassut had got to the story of the sheep (of which Cingar rids the boat by throwing overboard the one he had bought with the result that all the others immediately followed suit), when he became aware of his visitor. Laying the book down on the table, he turned towards the draper with a pleasant smile.

He asked after the health of his wife and his father-in-law and made all sorts of boring jokes about his recently-entered state of matrimony. The young man took advantage of this to bring up the subject of his misadventure. Having related the story of his quarrel with the arquebusier and encouraged by the magistrate's paternal manner, he confessed to its unhappy conclusion.

The magistrate looked at him with the same amazement as if he had been the good giant Fracasse in his book, or the faithful Falquet who had the hind-quarters of a greyhound, instead of Maître Eustache Bouteroue, shopkeeper of the Halles colonnade. Although news had reached him that Eustache was under suspicion, he had been unable to attach any credence to the report of a feat of arms in which a sword that pinned to the ground one of the king's soldiers had been wielded by a counter jumper no taller than Gribouille or Triboulet.

However, when he could no longer doubt the truth of the matter, he assured the poor draper that he would do everything in his power to keep it quiet and throw the men of justice off his scent. He promised him that unless the seconds accused him, he could soon live in peace, safe from the rope necklace.

Maître Chevassut even accompanied him to the door, repeating his assurances, but at the moment when he was about to make a graceful bow of farewell, Eustache took it into his head to administer a slap to the magistrate's face hard enough to rearrange his features, a glorious slap that gave him a countenance that was half red and half blue like the arms of the city of Paris and left him, to use the words of the immortal Rabelais, as *astounded as a bell founder*, opening his mouth in a great gape and as incapable of speech as a fish deprived of its tongue. Poor Eustache was so horrified that he fell down at Maître Chevassut's feet and begged pardon for his irreverence in the most penitent terms and with the most pitiful protestations, swearing that it was some unexpected completely involuntary convulsive spasm, and that he hoped the magistrate would be merciful. The old man helped him up, more astonished than angry, but scarce was he on his feet than Eustache gave him a second blow with the back of the hand, so hard that the five fingers left an impression you could have used as a mould.

This time, it had become unbearable and Maître Chevassut ran to the bell to call his servants, but the draper pursued him, continuing the performance. This spectacle was all the more extraordinary because every time he bestowed on his protector a masterly blow, Eustache accompanied the gesture with tearful excuses and stifled entreaties, the contrast being exceptionally amusing. In vain did he attempt to prevent the outbursts into which he was dragged by the hand: he was like a child who holds, by a thread attached to its claw, some great bird which pulls the child all over the room. Terrified, he dare not let go but is not strong enough to hold it still. And so the wretched Eustache was dragged by his hand in pursuit of the Lieutenant Civil who went round and round the chairs and tables, ringing and shouting, outraged and in pain. At last the servants entered the room, seized hold of Eustache Bouteroue and beat him to the ground where he collapsed in a dead faint. Maître Chevassut, who had no belief whatsoever in white magic could only think that he had been abused and mistreated by the young man for some reason he could not explain. He sent for the constables to whom he abandoned Eustache on a double charge of murder in the course of a duel and grievous bodily harm to a magistrate in his own home. Eustache only came round from his faint at the sound of the bolts opening the door of the cell allotted him.

'I am innocent!' he cried to the gaoler who was pushing him in.

'For heavens sake!' said the latter, 'Where do you think you are? They all say that here'.

XII
Death and Albertus Magnus

Eustache had been taken down to one of the cells of the Châtelet of which Cyrano said that it looked like a candlestick surmounted by a suction cup.

'If I were given this garment of rock for a coat it would be too big' he said after looking in every nook and cranny with a single pirouette, 'and if I had it for a tomb it would be too small. The lice here have teeth longer than their bodies and all the time you suffer from the stone, no less painful for being external'.

Our hero was able to reflect at leisure on his bad luck and curse the fatal gift of the gipsy who had seduced one of his limbs away from the natural authority of his head, resulting in all kinds of disorders. And so, great was his surprise when one day the gypsy calmly entered his cell and asked him how he was.

'May the devil hang you by the guts for your accursed magic, evil braggart and caster of spells!'

'What do you mean?' replied he, 'Is it my fault

you did not come on the tenth day to break the spell by bringing me the agreed sum of money?'

'How did I know you needed the money so soon?' said Eustache with a little less confidence. 'You can make gold whenever you want, like Flamel the alchemist.'

'Not true!' said the other, 'Quite the contrary. I will eventually master the great secret art and I am already well on the way to it, but so far I have only been able to turn fine gold into a very pure iron, a secret that the great Raymond Lulle discovered towards the end of his days'.

'How clever you are!' said the draper. 'So you have come to get me out of here at last. Excellent. And I no longer expected it...'

'That's the problem, my lad... I expect to be able to open doors without keys one of these days and you will see how we set about it...'

With these words the gypsy pulled his Albertus Magnus out of his pocket and by the light of the lantern he had brought with him he read out the following paragraph:

<u>*Heroic method whereby villains may enter houses*</u>
Take the hand cut from a hanged man which you must buy from him before his death. Plunge it,

taking care to keep it almost closed, into a copper vessel containing zimax and saltpetre with spondillis grease. Expose the vessel to a clear fire of bracken and verbena so that after a quarter of an hour the hand is perfectly dry and fit to be kept for a long time. Then, having made a candle from the fat of a sea calf and sesame oil from Laponia, use the hand as a holder for the candle when you have lit it. Wherever you go, if you hold it before you, bars will fall, locks will open and everyone you meet will stand still.

The hand prepared in this way is called a hand of glory.

'What a remarkable invention!' exclaimed Eustache Bouteroue.

'Listen: although you have not sold me your hand it belongs to me because you never redeemed it on the agreed date. The proof is that when the time had expired it behaved (because of the spirit by which it is possessed) in such a way that I could have the use of it later. Tomorrow you will be condemned to be hanged; the day after, the sentence will be carried out and the same evening I will harvest the highly prized fruit and treat it in the way prescribed.'

'Oh no you won't' cried Eustache. 'Tomorrow I will tell the authorities all about it.'

'Just you try: you will be burnt alive for using magic, which will prepare you in advance for the Devil's skewer... but that will not happen because your horoscope shows the gallows and nothing can change it.'

The wretched Eustache began to weep such bitter tears it was a piteous sight.

'There there, my friend,' said Maître Gonin gently, 'why rail against your destiny?'

'Good God, it's easy for you to say that,' sobbed Eustache, 'But when death is so close...'

'What is so amazing about death? I don't give a fig for it. *No one dies before his time*, says Seneca. Are you death's only vassal? Death respects no one. It is so bold it condemns, kills and seizes without distinction popes, emperors and kings as well as provosts, constables and other riff-raff. Do not be distressed at what comes sooner or later to everyone. Their condition is worse than yours, for if death is an ill, it is only an ill for those who are going to die. You only have one more day of that ill left and most of the others have twenty or thirty years or more. One of the Ancients has said: *The hour that gave you life has already diminished it.* You are in death while you are in life because when you are no longer alive you are *after* death. In other words, death does not concern you, dead or alive, because when you are alive you exist and when you are dead you no longer exist. Let this reasoning suffice to encourage you to drink the bitter draught without pulling a wry face and ponder the words of Lucretius in this fine verse which I quote: *Live as long as you can, you will take nothing away from the eternity of your own death.*

Having uttered these fine maxims, taken quintessentially from the ancient and modern and distilled to suit popular taste, Maître Gonin picked up his lantern and knocked on the cell door which the gaoler opened to let him out into the street. Darkness came down again on the prisoner like a leaden pall.

XIII
Where the Author Speaks

People who wish to know all the details of the trial of Eustache Bouteroue will find them in the *Memorable Judgments of the Parliament of Paris*, located in the library of manuscripts where Monsieur Paris will help them in their research with his customary kindness. The trial comes in alphabetical order before that of the Baron de Boutteville which is also very interesting because of the unusual nature of his duel with the Marquis de Bussi. The better to flout the edicts on duelling, he journeyed specially from Lorraine to Paris and fought his duel in the place Royale itself at three in the afternoon of Easter day, 1627. But these matters do not concern us. In the trial of Eustache Bouteroue we are only concerned with the duel and the outrage done to the Lieutenant Civil and not with the magic spell that caused the unfortunate series of events. But a note added to the documents refers the reader to the *Collection of Tragic Histories* by Belleforest (Edition de la Haye, the Rouen edition being incomplete). It is there we find those details which remain to be given about this story which Belleforest aptly entitled *The Demonic Hand*.

XIV
Conclusion

On the morning of his execution, Eustache, who

had been moved to a cell better lit than the first, received the visit of a priest who offered him a few crumbs of spiritual consolation in no better taste than those of the gypsy and which produced little effect. The priest was a tonsured individual from one of those excellent families where one of the children is always a man of the cloth. He wore an embroidered shirt front, his beard was waxed and drawn into a spindle point and he sported a moustache of the sort known as 'tusks', most elegantly turned up. His hair was very curly and he rolled his r's in an affected kind of way. Noting his frivolous and elegant appearance, Eustache did not have the heart to confess all his sins to him; he did so privately, to himself, to obtain forgiveness.

The priest gave him absolution and to occupy the time, as he had to stay with the condemned man until two o'clock, he gave him a book entitled *Tears of the Penitent Soul, or The Return of the Sinner to God*. Eustache opened the book at the royal *imprimatur* and started to read with solemn concentration, beginning with: *Henry, King of Navarre, to our loyal subjects, etc.*, till he arrived at the phrase: *For these reasons, regarding favourably the aforementioned petitioner....* At this point he could not help bursting into tears and he returned the book saying it was too touching and he was afraid he would be terribly upset if he read any more, so the priest produced a very handsome pack of cards from his pocket and invited the penitent to join him in a game or two in the course of which he lost the small sum of money Javotte had given him to purchase a few comforts. The poor man did not have his mind on the game and it is true to say he cared little about losing the money.

At two o'clock he was led trembling from the Châtelet, gabbling the Lord's prayer, and arrived at the place des Augustins between the two arcades which mark the entrance to the rue Dauphine and the beginning of the Pont Neuf where he was favoured with the provision of a stone gibbet. He showed commendable fortitude as he climbed the ladder, for a crowd had gathered to watch as this was one of the most frequently-used places of execution. However, as one always seeks to prolong the moment before taking the big jump, while the executioner was preparing to put the rope round his neck with as much ceremony as if it were the Golden Fleece (for men of that profession usually execute their duties with much skill and style) Eustache asked him to be kind enough to stop a moment so he could say another two prayers, to Saint Ignatius and Saint Louis of Gonzaga. He had kept these two till last as they had only been beatified in 1609. The man replied that the spectators had work to attend to and it was inconvenient to keep them waiting for such a modest spectacle as a mere hanging so he cut short Eustache's reply as he pushed him off the ladder. It was said that when everything was over and the executioner was on his way home, Maître Gonin appeared at one of the windows of the Château Gaillard looking out onto the square.

Immediately, although the draper's body was perfectly still and apparently inanimate, his arm came up and his hand waved joyously, like the tail of a dog greeting his master. A prolonged murmur of surprise arose among the spectators and those who were already on their way home rushed back like people who thought the play was over when there is still an act to go.

The executioner brought back the ladder, felt the feet of the hanged man behind his ankles: there was no pulse. He cut an artery but there was no blood yet the arm continued to make jerky movements. The man in red was not deterred. He climbed up on to the shoulders of his victim as the onlookers hissed and jeered but the hand treated his pimply face with the same irreverence it had shown to Maître Chevassut with the result that he drew from beneath his clothing, with an oath, a great knife he always had about him and with two blows cut off the demon hand. It made a prodigious leap and fell, all covered in blood, into the midst of the crowd which recoiled in horror. Then, springing about on its agile fingers it soon found itself at the foot of the tower of the Château Gaillard as the crowd made way for it. Hanging on by its fingers, like a crab, to the projections and cracks in the wall, it climbed up to the window where the gypsy was waiting.

Belleforest's account stops at this point and ends with these words: 'This occurrence, enlarged, commented and illustrated, was for a long time the subject of conversation among persons of quality as well as the populace, ever agog to hear stories of the weird and supernatural; but of course it may be one of those tales children love to hear as they sit by the fire, and not to be repeated by sensible people'.

THE DISAPPEARANCE OF HONORE SUBRAC

by Guillaume Apollinaire
First published in *L'Hérésiarque et cie,*
1910

THE DISAPPEARANCE OF HONORÉ SUBRAC

by Guillaume Apollinaire

First published in LES SOIRÉES DE PARIS
1910

THE DISAPPEARANCE OF HONORE SUBRAC

Notwithstanding the most painstaking enquiries, the police have been unable to solve the mystery of the disappearance of Honoré Subrac.

He was my friend, and as I know the truth about the case, I felt in duty bound to report what I knew to the authorities. After listening to my story, the magistrate who took down my evidence turned on me a look of such polite alarm I had no trouble in realising he took me for a madman. I told him so and he became even more polite, then rising to his feet he propelled me towards the door and I noticed that his clerk who had got up and had his fists clenched, was preparing to tackle me in case I turned violent.

I did not insist. The case of Honoré Subrac is, indeed, so strange that the truth seems unbelievable. The newspaper reports disclosed that Subrac was a well known eccentric. Winter and summer alike he wore only a greatcoat and a pair of slippers. He was very rich, so the simplicity of his attire surprised and amazed me. I asked the reason for it.

'It is so that I can undress more quickly when the need arises' he answered. 'In the meantime, you get used to going out with not much on. You can easily do without underwear, socks, and hat. I've been doing this since I was twenty-five and am none the worse for it.'

Instead of enlightening me, these words aroused my curiosity even more.

'Why does Honoré Subrac need to get undressed so quickly?' I asked myself. And I made a great many suppositions...

* *
*

One night when I was returning home at about one o'clock, perhaps a quarter past, I heard someone utter my name in a low voice. It seemed to come from the wall. I stopped, disagreeably surprised.

'Is there anyone else in the street?' continued the voice. 'It's me, Honoré Subrac'.

'Where are you?' I cried, looking all round with no idea where my friend was hiding. I merely noticed his famous greatcoat lying on the pavement next to his no less renowned slippers.

'This is one of those occasions when Honoré Subrac has been obliged to undress in a flash', I said to myself. 'I am about to fathom a great mystery'.

I said aloud: 'The street is empty, dear friend. You can appear!'

Suddenly Honoré Subrac detached himself in some way from the wall where I had not seen him standing. He was stark naked and hurriedly put on his overcoat buttoning it up hastily. Then he put on his slippers, and speaking very deliberately, addressed me thus as he accompanied me to my front door:

'You were surprised', he said, 'but now you understand why I dress so strangely. What you don't understand, however, is how I could have disappeared so completely from your sight. It's very simple, a phenomenon of *mimesis*, that's all. Nature is a good mother: she has granted to those of her children who are too weak to defend themselves the gift of merging with their surroundings. You know all about that, of course - you know that butterflies resemble flowers, some insects are like leaves, the chameleon can assume the colour that disguises it best and the arctic hare has become as white as the icy lands where, as timid as our own native species, it can take flight almost invisibly.

'This is how those vulnerable creatures escape their enemies - by an instinctive reflex action which changes their appearance.

'I am like those creatures. I am constantly pursued, but timid and incapable of defending myself in a fight. I can merge at will with my surroundings when I am afraid. I first discovered this knack a number of years ago when I was twenty-five. Generally speaking, women found me attractive, and a certain married woman showed so much interest in me I was unable to resist. Unhappy liaison! One night I was with my lover when her husband was away for a few days, or so we thought. We were as naked as Adam and Eve when the door opened suddenly and the husband appeared with a revolver in his hand. My terror was indescribable and I had but one desire, coward that I was and still am: the desire to disappear. As I stood there with my back to the wall, I wished to become indistinguishable from it and immediately my wish was granted! I became the colour of the wallpaper, my limbs flattened themselves in an amazing involuntary shrinking movement and I seemed to be part and parcel of the wall. No one could see me! With murder in his heart, the husband searched high and low about the room. He had already seen me and it was impossible I could have escaped. He went berserk, turned his rage against his wife, brutally killed her by firing six bullets into her head. Then he went away, weeping uncontrollably. As soon as he had gone, my body resumed its normal shape and colour. I dressed and managed to escape before anyone came. Since that day I have continued to possess this remarkable ability. The husband devoted the rest of his life to tracking me down - he has pursued me all over the world and when I came to Paris I thought I had escaped him at last. But just before you happened along I caught sight of him again. My teeth were chattering and I only just had time to undress and merge with the wall. He passed me, gazing curiously at this greatcoat and these slippers lying on the pavement - you see how right I am to dress scantily: my *mimetic* faculty would not succeed if I was dressed like everyone else because I couldn't get undressed quickly enough to escape my tormentor and above all I must be naked so that my clothes flattened against the wall don't give me away.'

I congratulated Subrac on the enviable power he had just demonstrated to me. For the next few days I was unable to think of anything else and constantly found myself trying by sheer force of will to change my own shape and colour. I tried to turn myself into a bus, into the Eiffel Tower, into a member of the Académie Française, into a lottery winner, but my efforts were in vain. My will was not strong enough and besides, I lacked that impulse of sheer mortal terror, that dreadful sense of danger which had aroused the instincts of Honoré Subrac...

* * *

I had not seen him for some time when he turned up one day terrified out of his wits.

'That man won't leave me alone. I've managed to get away three times already but I can't go on much longer. What can I do?'

I could see that he had lost a lot of weight but refrained from mentioning it.

'There's only one thing you can do,' I said. 'You will only escape such a pitiless enemy by losing yourself in some remote village or other. Leave me to take care of your affairs and head for the nearest station.'

Grasping my hand, he pleaded: 'Come with me, please. Don't leave me - I'm so frightened!'

* *
*

In silence we walked down the street together. Honoré Subrac kept turning his head round anxiously. Suddenly he uttered a cry of alarm and began to run, at the same time removing his greatcoat and slippers. A man came running up behind us. He was holding a revolver aimed in the general direction of Honoré Subrac. The latter had just reached the long wall of a neighbouring barracks when he disappeared as if by magic.

The man with the revolver stopped in amazement, emitted a howl of rage and as if to take revenge upon the wall which seemed to have snatched his victim away from him discharged his revolver into the very spot at which Subrac had disappeared. Then he took off at a run.

A crowd began to form and policemen arrived to disperse it. Then I called my friend's name but there was no reply.

I felt the wall. It was still warm and I noticed that of the six shots three had impacted at the height of a man's heart whilst the others had skimmed the plaster, higher up, just where I thought I could vaguely distinguish the outline of a face...

CHRONOLOGIES
1. Théophile Gautier
2. Gérard de Nerval
3. Guillaume Apollinaire

Théophile Gautier
Chronology

1811   Born at Tarbes. Father is a senior civil servant.
1815   The family moves to Paris
1822   Attends the Collège Louis le Grand then the Collège Royal de Charlemagne where he meets Gérard de Nerval. Both young men share literary enthusiasms such as Hoffmann. They remained friends for life and later used their combined initials 'G.G.' for joint theatre reviews.
1829   Gautier is introduced by Nerval to Victor Hugo.
1830   He takes part in the famous battle of *Hernani*, Hugo's play which divided opinion into classic v. romantic and ended in uproar, Gautier joined in enthusiastically on the side of the Romantics, prominent in his extravagant dress and great mop of hair. His first collection of poems is published, including *Albertus*.
1831   Story, *La Cafetière*.
1832   *La Comédie de la mort* (poetry).

1834 Omphale.
1836 Travels in Belgium with Nerval
Writes *Mademoiselle de Maupin*
Meets Eugénie Fort who becomes his mistress; birth of a son, Théophile.
Gautier refuses to marry Eugénie and fights a duel with her brother.
La Morte Amoureuse.
Begins a long period of on-going work for different journals, notably *La Presse* (until 1856) and *Le Moniteur.*
1840 Travels in Spain. Gautier's many foreign excursions were financed by literary journals which published his travel writing.
Le Chevalier Double.
Le Pied de Momie.
Meets Carlotta Grisi, the dancer, for whom he writes the ballet *Giselle.*
1843 Begins liaison with Ernesta Grisi, sister of Carlotta. Less flamboyant than her sister, she is a moderately successful singer. Gautier lives with her for more than twenty years and they have two daughters, Judith and Estelle.

1845 Travels in Algeria.
Publishes collection of complete verse.
1850 Joins Marie Mattei in Italy. Brief liaison.
1851 Travels to London for the Great Exhibition.
1852 Travels in Constantinople, Athens, Venice. Writes *Arria Marcella*.
His most famous collection of verse, *Emaux et Camées*, appears this year.
1854 Visits Germany.
1856 *Avatar* (Story)
1857 *Le Roman de la Momie*.
1858 Goes to Russia with the photographer Richeburg. They plan a book for the series *Trésors d'Art* (incomplete).
1863 Publishes *Le Capitaine Fracasse*.
1869 Travels in Egypt for the opening of the Suez Canal.
1870 Siege of Paris in Franco-Prussian War.
1871 Stays in Brussels and Geneva.
1872 Dies in Paris of heart disease aggravated by the stress of the siege.
Tableaux de Siège is published - description of life in Paris during the siege.

Gérard de Nerval Chronology

1808 Born in Paris, son of Dr Etienne Labrunie and Marie-Antoinette, née Laurent.
Gérard is brought up in the Valois region, in Paris and in Saint Germain until his father returns from service with Napoleon's army.

1810 Death of Gérard's mother.

1814 Dr Labrunie settles at 72, rue Saint Martin, Paris.

1822 Gérard attends the Collège Royal de Charlemagne, 1822-1827, where he meets Gautier.
His father wishes him to become a doctor; Gérard is unwilling.

1826 First ventures into poetry : writes *Napoleon et la France Guerrière, La Mort de Talma, Napoléon et Talma, L'Académie ou les Membres introuvables.*

1827 *Elégies nationales* et *Satires politiques.*
Writes a new translation in prose and verse of Goethe's *Faust* : this is used by Berlioz in his *Eight Scenes from Faust*

1829 He contributes to the *Mercure de France.*

1830 Translates German poetry : Klopstock, Goethe, Schiller.

Compiles a selection of early French poetry.

1831 *Nicholas Flamel; Odelettes.*

1832 *La Main de Gloire,* later renamed *La Main Enchantée*

1834 Inherits 30,000 francs from his grandfather.
Travels in the south of France and Italy.

1835 Founds a journal, *le Monde dramatique.*
Adopts the pseudonym Gérard de Nerval.

1836 *Le Monde dramatique* is sold. He is in debt. Travels with Gautier in Belgium.

1837-38 Contributes to various journals. *Piquillo* is produced at the Opéra Comique with the actress Jenny Colon, for whom he conceives a violent but apparently unrequited passion.
Travels in the East of France and Germany with Dumas.

1839 *L'Alchimiste* and *Léo Burckart.* In Vienna he meets Marie Pleyel at the French Embassy.

1840 Takes Gautier's place as contributor to *La Presse* (theatre magazine).
3rd edition of his translation of Goethe's *Faust.*

Travels in Belgium where he again meets Marie Pleyel and Jenny Colon.
1841 First mental breakdown. Placed in the *maison de santé* of Dr Blanche who advises him against writing.
1842 Death of Jenny Colon.
Les Vieilles Ballades Françaises
De Nerval leaves for travels in the near East.
1843 Visits Alexandria, Cairo, Beyrouth, Constantinople, Malta.
Returns to Paris.
1844 Contributes to *L'Artiste;* articles on his journeys in the Middle East.
1845 Writes for *La Presse*.
Le Temple d'Isis.
Souvenir de Pompeii.
1846 *Les Femmes du Caire* published in the *Revue des Deux Mondes*.
Brief stay in London where he meets Marie Pleyel again.
His co-authorship of the libretto for *Faust* is acknowledged.
1848 *Scènes de la Vie Orientale*.
1851 *Voyage en Orient*.

1852 Further breakdown requiring entry into the *maison municipale de santé,* 110 rue du Faubourg Saint Denis.
Journey to Holland and Belgium.
Publication of *Les Illuminés, Fêtes de mai en Hollande, Lorely.*
Souvenirs d'Allemagne, La Bohème Galante, Nuits d'octobre and *Contes et Facéties,* in which *La main de Gloire* is included.

1853 Publication of *Petits Châteaux de Bohème.*
Hospitalization at 110 rue du Faubourg Saint Denis.
Sylvie published in the *Revue des Deux Mondes.*
Further mental breakdown; de Nerval is admitted to Dr Blanche's clinic in Passy.

1854 Publication of *Les Filles du Feu.*
De Nerval leaves the clinic of Dr Blanche against the latter's advice.
First instalments of *Pandora* and *Promenades et Souvenirs*, in *Le Mousquetaire* and *L'Illustration.*

1855 First instalment of *Aurélia* in the *Revue de Paris.*

Nerval is found hanged from a lamp-post in the rue de la Vieille Lanterne, near the Châtelet.
His funeral service is held at Notre Dame de Paris and he is buried at Père Lachaise. Later that year, *L'Illustration* publishes another two chapters of *Promenades et Souvenirs* and the *Revue de Paris* publishes the second part of *Aurélia* which is the account of Nerval's personal descent into hell during a period of insanity.

Guillaume Apollinaire Chronology

1880 Born in Rome to Angelica de Kostrowitsky. Father unknown. Guillaume attends the Collège Saint Charles at Monaco where his mother works at the Casino as an *entraîneuse*, or dance hostess.

1896 He transfers to the Collège Stanislas in Cannes.

1897 Again transfers, to the French Lycée in Nice.
The family of Madame Kostrowitsky, Guillaume and his younger brother Albert leave Monaco for Stavelot in Eastern Belgium; some time later they leave Stavelot under a cloud, having failed to settle the hotel bill.

1899 The family moves to Paris. Guillaume takes various ill-paid jobs, meanwhile writing stories and poetry.

1901 He has three poems published in *La Grande France*.
Guillaume leaves France for Honnef-on-

Rhine where he is employed as a tutor to the daughter of the Vicomtesse de Milhau. He falls in love with the girl's English governess, Annie Playden.

1903 He is employed in Paris as a bank clerk. He contributes stories, poems and articles to the *Revue Blanche* and *l'Européen*. At about this time he begins to call himself Guillaume Apollinaire. (Michal Apollinaris Kostrowitsky was his grandfather's name.) Travels to London where he proposes to Annie Playden but is refused. The poem *Chanson du Mal Aimé* reflects his rejection by Annie. Apollinaire attends the Soirées de la Plume where poets meet to read and discuss their work.

1904 He meets the artists Vlaminck and Derain, the poet Max Jacob. Writes *L'Emigrant de Landor Road.*

1905 Apollinaire meets Picasso at one of the English Bars at the Gare St Lazare. Writes about Picasso in *La Revue Immoraliste*; article in *La Plume* about Picasso's paintings of harlequins and children.

Picasso introduces him to the painter Marie Laurencin, the love of his life. The end of their relationship gave rise, later, to the fine poem *Sous le Pont Mirabeau coule la Seine.*

1906 Apollinaire makes money out of erotic extravaganzas *Les Onze Mille Verges* and *Exploits d'un jeune don Juan*, the former of eyebrow-raising audacity, even a hundred years later. Revenue from these enables him to escape from the boring routine of clerking and he finds a new career in the cataloguing of the so-called *'Enfer'*, the locked collection of erotica in the Bibliothèque Nationale. Although it was unauthorised, Apollinaire's catalogue was so scrupulously compiled it is still in use at the Bibliothèque Nationale.

1909 Publication of *L'Enchanteur Pourrissant,* with wood-cuts by Derain.

1910 Publication of *L'Hérésiarque et cie* a collection of short stories. It is proposed for the Prix Goncourt.

1911 Publication of *Le Bestiaire*, wood-cuts by

Raoul Dufy. This beautiful production, in a limited edition, is now highly prized by bibliophiles although about half remained unsold and had to be remaindered.

This was the year of the disappearance from the Louvre of the *Mona Lisa*. Apollinaire came under suspicion because he had befriended (and used as the model for a character in *L'Hérésiarque*, the Baron d'Ormeson) a certain Géry Piéret who had preciously stolen some ancient stone heads from the Louvre and passed them on to Picasso. The heads were eventually returned to the Louvre via the offices of *Paris-Journal*, which ran a story on art thefts.

The police suspected Piéret of being involved in an international gang of art thieves. After searching Apollinaire's apartment in Auteuil, where they found correspondence from Piéret, the police arrested Apollinaire on a charge of harbouring a criminal. Apollinaire was released after spending five days in the Santé prison, an experience which affected him deeply.

In fact, Piéret had nothing to do with the disappearance of the *Mona Lisa* which was recovered in Florence in 1913. An Italian painter and decorator, Vincenzo Peruggia, who had once worked at the Louvre, had stolen it 'to restore the picture to its native land.'

1912 Marie Laurencin finally breaks with Apollinaire. She married in 1914 and spent the war years with her husband in Spain. Apollinaire never saw her again. Apollinaire is invited to co-edit a series called *Soirées de Paris.*

1913 Publication of *Alcools*, a collection of fifty-five poems, 1898-1913.

1914 Outbreak of war. Apollinaire enlists in the 38th Artillery Regiment. A fearless and energetic soldier, Apollinaire is commissioned lieutenant. His war poems of this period reflect the picturesque aspects of combat - 'Dieu, que la guerre est jolie'.

He meets Lou, Louise de Coligny - Châtillon, to whom 76 poems are addressed. Their affair ends with regret on Apollinaire's part, having been conducted intermittently during A's war service.

The *Lettres à Lou* written at this time were published by Gallimard in 1969, with the poems.

1915 Meets Madeleine Pagès on a train from Nice to Marseilles and becomes engaged to her, whilst continuing to see Lou. The exchange of letters and poems with Madeleine provide a release from the stresses of the battlefield.

1916 Apollinaire is wounded in the head by a splinter while sitting in a trench reading the *Mercure de France*. He had just been granted French nationality.

The splinter was removed in a field hospital, but a trepanning operation was later performed to relieve pressure on the brain which had caused loss of power in his left arm. Though successful, the operation left him very depressed. Apollinaire breaks off the relationship with Madeleine Pagès to whom he had become engaged.

Writes a satirical drama, *Les Mamelles de Tirésias*. The poet himself called it a 'drama surréaliste', using that now famous word, which he coined for the first time. *'Le Poète assassiné'* a prose extravaganza, is published.

1918 Publishes *Calligrammes*, over a hundred poems in the shape of pictures, 1913-16. 2 May, marries Jacqueline Kolb. 9 November, dies of influenza. He is buried in Père Lachaise. Madame de Kostrowisky and Guillaume's brother Albert both died a few months later.

1959 Monument erected to the memory of Apollinaire in the Square Laurent-Prache, at the corner of the Place Saint-Germain - des Prés and the rue de l'Abbaye.

GLOSSARY

PART 1, Théophile Gautier
PART 2, Gerard de Nerval

PART I (Théophile Gautier)

AGUADO, Alexandre.

Born at Seville in Spain in 1784, he began life as a soldier, fighting with distinction in the Spanish War of Independence on the side of Joseph Bonaparte. After the battle of Beylen (1808) he entered the French army in which he rose to become colonel and aide-de-camp to Marshal Soult. Exiled in 1851, he became a commission agent in Paris where, through family connections in Havana and Mexico he acquired enough wealth to take up banking. Negotiating several loans for the Spanish government, he was rewarded by Ferdinand Vll with the title of Marquis de las Marismas del Guadalquivir, Viscount of Monte Ricco. He also received mining rights in Spain. Naturalized French in 1828 he purchased large estates including the famed Chateau Margaux with its wine interests. Aguado died in 1842, leaving a fortune estimated at 60,000,000 francs and a large collection of pictures acquired by the French government and later placed in the Louvre, referred to by Gautier in the *The Mummy's Foot*.

BOUCHER, Francois

Born in Paris, 1703. Boucher painted pastoral and mythological scenes, graceful and decorative in character. He was the most typical of the rococo artists. Madame de Pompadour, mistress of Louis XV, was his friend and patron. He produced many tapestry designs including the *Rising and Setting of the Sun,* 1753, which, with other examples of his best work, are in the Wallace Collection. Boucher died in 1770.

CANDIDE

Eponymous hero of Voltaire's novel, 1759. An innocent inexperienced youth, he has many unfortunate adventures before coming to the conclusion that all is not for the best in the best of all possible worlds.

CLEOPATRA

In *The Amorous Dead* Gautier more than once mentions Clarimonde and Cleopatra in the same breath. The 'abominations' with which the abbé Serapion associates the Egyptian queen refer to Cleopatra's last days. Her lover Anthony's troops had been defeated by Octavian at Actium which meant their days were numbered, so they were said, according to Petrarch, to have formed a society at Alexandria where the members prepared to die together, spending their remaining time in orgies and feasting before committing suicide.

COUNCIL OF TEN
Referred to in *The Amorous Dead,* the Council of Ten in Venice was erected first as a temporary committee of public safety to deal with the conspiracy led by one Bajamonte Tiepolo. After the conspiracy had been scotched the committee hunted down the last few of its members. It was made permanent in 1335. It met in secret and could act rapidly when circumstances required. The Council gradually absorbed many more of the functions of state and as well as dealing with all cases of conspiracy it exercised considerable power in criminal jurisdiction. It was in communication with envoys abroad and its orders would override those of the senate.

FOSCARI
A well-known noble Venetian family. Foscari, 1373-1457 became doge of Venice in 1423 and

reigned for thirty-four years. His son Jacopo brought disgrace to the family name, dying in exile in 1457. The grief-stricken father died shortly afterwards. Byron wrote a tragedy on the subject in 1821 and Verdi composed an opera entitled *I due Foscari*.

OMPHALE
In ancient Greek legend she was the wife of Tmolus, king of Lydia after whose death she reigned as queen. As an atonement for the murder of Iphitus, Hercules had to become her servant for a period of three years during which time he is said to have used the distaff and spun wool, wearing women's clothes, while Omphale put on his lion skin and bore his club. In Gautier's story the role reversal by which Omphale assumes a travesty of masculinity is echoed by the dominant role of the marquise in the relationship.

OSIRIS
According to legend, Osiris was a wise and beneficent king of Egypt whose reign was brought to a premature end by the machinations of his brother Seth who with seventy-two fellow

conspirators invited him to a banquet, induced him to enter a cunningly-wrought coffin made exactly to his measure then shut down the lid and cast it into the Nile. Isis, the faithful wife of Osiris, set forth in search of her husband's body, recovered it and brought it back to Egypt. Seth gained possession of the corpse, however, and while Isis was absent on a visit to her son, cut it into fourteen pieces and scattered them all over Egypt. But Isis collected the pieces and by virtue of her magic powers joined them together again and made the resurrected Osiris King of the Nether Regions. Gautier's display of knowledge about Pharaonic Egypt is a reminder that at the time he wrote *The Mummy's Foot* there was a great surge of interest in Egyptology.

PALISSY, Bernard

Bernard Palissy, 1510-1589, was born near Agen in SW France. After working as a glass painter he settled at Saintes. He discovered a process for the manufacture of fine enamel after labouring for sixteen years until he achieved success. He was arrested as a Huguenot in 1562 but released by royal command, his work having come to the attention of the king, and he was permitted to build his pottery works close to the Tuileries. Although escaping the massacre of Saint Bartholomew he was arrested and imprisoned in the Bastille in 1585, never after to be released. One of the most respected natural scientists of his day, he lectured to large audiences in Paris from 1575 to 1584.

He never used the wheel and his best-known pieces were made by moulding and finished by modelling. Large plates and dishes are decorated with realistic figures of reptiles, shells, fish, plants, etc. They excel in the sharpness of the modelling and their subdued richness of colour. Collections are to be found in the V and A, the British Museum and the Wallace Collection, as well as in the Louvre.

REGENCY

Philip, Duke of Orleans, son of Louis XlV's brother *Monsieur* presided over a period which was in reaction against the stuffiness of the Sun King's final years. The Regent embodied the spirit of his age. The late Professor Ritchie wrote of that period: '*La vie parisienne* is a phenomenon difficult to define but it is at least one to which precise dates can be assigned. It was inaugurated in 1715, it ended for a time in 1789 and Philip was one of its first and most brilliant exponents. The luxury trades revived. The entertainment industry prospered. The fine arts flourished as never before. The painters were working for patrons less pompous than the lords and ladies of the court. Fermiers Généraux, capitalists, parvenus, had their portraits painted as humble folk today have themselves photographed. Their town houses were enlivened with wall panels depicting the new and brighter conception of what a happy life should be'. Gautier's descriptions of the bedroom in *The Coffee Pot* and the pavilion in *Omphale*. recreate that atmosphere. A certain nostalgia for the period creeps into Gautier's evocation of Regency taste and manners.

ROCOCO

Rococo and *rocaille* both derive from the French for rock. *Rocaille* means any object whose lines recall the shapes of rocks and shells. *Rococo* was invented later by artists making fun of the *rocaille* manner. Like other elements of the *Ancien Regime* which became pejorative expressions, *rocaille* and *rococo* meant old-fashioned and quaint. Today the word means 18th century in style but at the time of Gautier it meant out-of-date and ridiculous like the decor of the uncle's pavilion in *Omphale* and possibly the uncle himself.

TUBAL CAIN
Referred to in *The Mummy's Foot*. He is the son of Lamech the biblical patriarch who appears in the antediluvian genealogies in Genesis IV, 16-24. Tubal Cain was the supposed ancestor of all metal workers, 'an instructor of every artificer in brass and iron.'

VANLOO Jean-Baptiste
Born in 1684 at Aix en Provence, Vanloo was a genre and portrait painter. He was highly esteemed as a portraitist, producing excellent likenesses which were seldom flattering. In 1737 he went to England where he became the protégé of Sir Robert Walpole and for a time there was even talk of his becoming official portrait painter to the Royal family, causing alarm and jealousy among the native artists. He returned to Paris in

1742 complaining that the English weather did not suit him and died in 1745. His portrait of Walpole hangs in the National Portrait Gallery.

WITZILIPUTZILI (Huitzilipochtoli)

Mexican war god, head of the Aztec pantheon. His idol can be seen in Mexico and is a huge block of basalt on which is sculptured on the one side his hideous likeness, adorned with humming bird feathers on the left hand which signify his name, while the equally frightful war goddess Teoyomiqui or 'divine war death' occupies the other side.

PART II (Gérard de Nerval)

ALBERTUS MAGNUS
Sorcerer and alchemist, author of *The Book of Secrets*

ARQUEBUSIER
Soldier armed with an arquebus or harquebus, the ancestor of the rifle. It was the first portable firearm, still in use in the 17th century.

D'AUBIGNY, Agrippa
Born 1552, an ardent Calvinist and companion in arms to Henry IV of France. He wrote *Les Tragiques* in 1661, followed by an epic, a universal history, a satirical novel, the *Adventures of Baron Funeste* and poems which are an early example of the literary baroque style.

GRANDS AUGUSTINS
Convent of the order of Saint Augustine which was near the Paris street which still bears its name.

BAND OF SAINT NICHOLAS
Also known as the 'Basoches' they were lawyers renowned for their verbal skill.

BERTRAND DE CLASQUIN
Neval uses a facetious form of the name Bertrand du Guesclin, Constable of France, 1315-1380, famed for his feats of arms.

BOOK OF THE SIX CORPORATIONS
There were six merchant guilds in Paris, but Nerval probably invented the title of the book.

BRUSCAMBILLE
A tooth-puller, famous for his verbal dexterity who became the compère of the theatre of the Hotel de Bourgogne.

CHATELET
Name given to two fortresses in Paris, the Grand and the Petit Chatelet. The first, demolished in 1802, was on the right bank of the Seine opposite the Pont au Change. It was the seat of jurisdiction of the city of Paris. The second, on the Left Bank, was used as a prison. It was demolished in 1782.

COCCAIE, Merlin
Italian Benedictine monk of the 16th century, poet of the Macaronic school. Balde, Cingar, Fracasse

and Falchetto are characters in the burlesque epic *Baldus* 1517, translated in 1606 under the title *Macaronic History of Merlin Coccaie* prototype of Rablais (sic).

CORNEILLE AGRIPPA
Author of *Occult Philosophy* 1727

COUR DES MIRACLES
A district of Paris situated between the rue Réaumur and the rue du Caire. It was in those days a retreat for beggars and vagabonds, described by Victor Hugo in *Notre Dame de Paris*.

COURS LA REINE
Avenue laid out in 1616 for Marie de Medicis, second wife of Henri IV.

ENFANTS SANS SOUCI
'Children without care' or *'Children of Fun'*. A very popular theatrical company founded c1380 and specialising in political satire. Its stage was in Les Halles. The leading actor was known as the 'Prince of Fools' and one such, Nicolas Joubert, known as Le Seigneur d' Engoulevent, was famous for winning, in 1608, a law-suit which led

to an Act of Parliament.

CHATEAU GAILLARD
Building about which little is known, still standing in the 17th century at the southern extremity of the Pont Neuf. Old engravings show a fortified building of mediaeval appearance; Nerval gives it a sinister aura as the dwelling of the magician Maître Gonin.

GALINETTE LA GALINE
Nickname of Hieronimo who sold ointment for burns on the Pont Neuf.

GASCONS
They were reputedly poor but courageous and became, in the writings of Alexandre Dumas, typical figures of quarrelsome bravery at the time of Louis Xlll. The Gascons are said to be great boasters.

MAITRE GONIN
A famous conjuror working from the Pont Neuf.

GRIBOUILLE
Character of folklore, clumsy and naive.

THE GUILLERIS BROTHERS
Breton highwaymen of the 17th century.

HAND OF GLORY
The name *Hand of Glory* is given to a hand cut from the corpse of a hanged criminal dried in smoke and used as a charm or talisman for the finding of treasure, etc. The French *Main de Gloire* is a corruption of the Old French mandegloire, i.e. mandragora, the mandrake, to the root of which many magic properties were attributed. Shakespeare more than once alludes to this plant, as in *Antony and Cleopatra*, 'Give me to drink mandragora.' The notion that the plant shrieked when touched is referred to in *Romeo and Juliet.* The mandrake, often growing like the lower limbs of a man was supposed to have other virtues and was much used for love philtres.

HENRY THE GREAT
Henry IV of France, 1553-1610, King of Navarre, 1562-1610 and of France 1589-1610. A Protestant, he converted to Catholicism in 1593. Henry overcame opposition within and without

the kingdom. The Edict of Nantes, 1598, ensured freedom from religious persecution. His reign was marked by agricultural and industrial progress as well as by overseas expansion; Quebec was founded in 1608. His second marriage to Marie de Médicis produced a son, later Lois Xlll. Henry was assassinated by Ravaillac in 1610.

MONSIEUR DE HUMIERES
A 17th century Marshal of France.

HUON DE BORDEAUX
One of the *chansons de geste*, epic or heroic poems of the 13th century.

CAPTAIN MATAMORES
Name of the cowardly braggart of Spanish comedy (literally, 'killer of Moors') Hero of Corneille's *L'lllusion Comique*, 1636. It quickly entered common usage.

LE MENTEUR
The Liar, comedy by Molière, 1662, The eponymous hero is seen by Nerval as a kind of toned-down Gascon.

PRE AUX CLERCS
Park land near St. Germain des Prés, rendezvous for the students of the University of Paris. François I gave part of it to the clerks of the Palais de Justice. It was built on towards the end of the 16th century.

THE SAMARITAINE
In 1608 Henri IV ordered the construction of the Samaritaine pump, demolished in 1813. A bronze group depicted Christ being given water by the woman of Samaria. There was a bell tower built over it, sounding the hours.

SPONDILLIS GREASE
A humorous invention of Nerval's. It suggests a mollusc or the bones of the spine (spondyles).

TAILLEBRAS
Type of cowardly warrior similar to Captain Matamores.

TABARIN, Antoine Girard
Born 1584, famous comic actor whose shows, full

of references to current affairs, helped to develop the burlesque as a theatrical genre. Tabarin died in 1633.

KING OF THUNES
King of the beggars. See Victor Hugo, *Notre Dame de Paris* part 2.

TOUR DE BOIS
This was on the Right Bank, on the site of the present-day Louvre.

TOUR DE NESLE
There were two Hotels de Nesle: one was situated where the Institut de France stands today, the other was on the site of Chamber of Commerce. Dumas set his play, *La Tour de Nesle* (1832) in the tower which was once part of the fortifications of Philip Augustus, opposite the tower of the Louvre.

TRIBOULET
A famous dwarf, the clown of Louis Xll and François 1.

THE ABBE TRITEME
German theologian, 15th century.

VILLON, François

Born Paris 1431, died c1463. First great French lyric poet, his work is inspired by the lives of humble people. His most famous poem, *Ballade des Dames du Temps Jadis,* has the well known line 'Where are the snows of yesteryear?' He was thought to have lived 'on the edge' and to have escaped the noose on more than one occasion.

The Freeloaders (Les Repues Franches) an anonymous poem of the late 15th century, was attributed to Villon.

ZIMAC

Mentioned in the *Dictionnaire de Trevaux* 1771: 'Term of alchemy, a green vitriol from which brass is made.'